POISON IVY

'She's death to men,' they told
trouble-buster Joe P. Heggy. And when
he knew her past . . . the men who'd
died for her . . . he tried to keep clear.
But she wouldn't let him. Then, when
a mob formed a manhunt, they
became the targets — their lives were
at stake, because of the fears and
jealousy of a craven power-seeker.
They endured a night of fear in the
mountains as they battled to survive,
and Heggy learned what made her
Poison Ivy.

GORDON LANDSBOROUGH

POISON IVY

Complete and Unabridged

LINFORD
Leicester

First published in Great Britain

First Linford Edition
published 2009

British Library CIP Data

Landsborough, Gordon.
  Poison Ivy - - (Linford mystery library)
  1. Suspense fiction.
  2. Large type books.
  I. Title II. Series
  823.9'14–dc22

  ISBN 978–1–84782–790–6

Published by
F. A. Thorpe (Publishing)
Anstey, Leicestershire

Set by Words & Graphics Ltd.
Anstey, Leicestershire
Printed and bound in Great Britain by
T. J. International Ltd., Padstow, Cornwall

This book is printed on acid-free paper

1

Murder on a mountain

Twin lights scythed a hole in the darkness. Our lights. The only thing on the road at that time of night.

Most of the time that hole was just hole, with nothing to reflect back light because there was just nothing that side of the twisty, turning, mountain road . . . just a damned great drop of several hundred feet over a precipice edge.

Occasionally we saw rocks lifting to our right, just occasionally a tree hardy enough to grow at this height. But most of the time we could only sit in terror, because there wasn't a one of us who thought we were going to come through that bus-ride alive, and we saw — nothing.

That wouldn't have been so bad, but it seemed to us our driver couldn't see anything, either. It didn't seem possible.

And yet he kept hauling on that wheel, throwing the old bus lurching round unseen bends, and he even had time to turn round occasionally and grin at us and declare: 'We'll hit Kyrenia any time, folks.'

It was what we were all afraid of. Kyrenia lay two thousand feet below, a dozen miles ahead on the northern shore of Cyprus. We didn't want to hit Kyrenia. We just wanted to get there in a nice, orthodox fashion.

Two people hated that large-thewn, khaki-shorted Cypriot driver. The other fellow was breathing in anguish down my neck.

He kept gasping: 'For God's sake, why did I ever get on this thing! We'll go over the drop any time now!'

I wouldn't look round at him. I was hanging out of the open window, the rush of hot night breeze whipping my hair almost off my skull. It was that kind of night. They have them a lot in Cyprus. Hot as hell, even after the sun's gone down, so that your clothes stick to you and you sweat, but the breeze doesn't cool you off at all.

The sort of night you get when a storm's beating up out of the sea. And there was a storm working up. We could see the vivid lightning in the northern distance and we all knew it was approaching fast.

That's why that Cypriot driver was taking risks on a road that zigzagged crazily down the rocky abruptness of a mighty mountain range. He wanted to reach Kyrenia before the rain came. To us, hurled about in that jiving old ruin called a bus, we didn't give a cuss about a bit of rain; it was that precipice by our nearside wheels that gave us the creeps.

Berny Gissenheim — the man who'd been my boss until a couple of hours back — was shouting: 'Get this thing stopped, Heggy. Why do we let a maniac drive us!'

That was what he was saying when we saw the fellow.

For one moment the lights didn't swing over that ghastly void. Instead they ripped apart the night's blackness along the length of steeply descending road. A man was momentarily revealed. As I was leaning out of the window, he looked squat and all white to me — but that's how they always look with headlights upon them.

He had his right hand raised, facing us. The lights missed him, then swung back again. Our Cypriot driver was standing on his brakes, but we were going fast, awfully fast. We would overshoot the guy, I saw at once.

And then I came standing up in my seat, the hair lifting on my scalp, my mouth opening and dry with horror.

For that lone man on that winding mountain trail seemed to fall sideways into the road right under our wheels.

I guess most of us in that bus saw it. We were all hanging out of the windows to get the benefit of the, in theory, cooling night air, and to see when death came jumping up at us.

Right when he was falling I thought a tyre had gone flat. There was a report and it just sounded like a blowout.

Then everything happened at once.

Our Cypriot driver was juggling frantically with that wheel. The bus was swaying all over the place. Everyone was trying to get to their feet, and there were screams and shouts of alarm.

Then the Cypriot driver was yelling his head off but gallantly sticking to his brakes. We seemed to go down over the front nearside wheel. There was an awful scraping sound and a jarring feeling through the framework of the bus.

Then we were stopped, but we were at such an angle we were almost falling down the length of the bus. The lights dimmed, and then fortunately held and didn't go out.

I saw that girl, the girl who had cost me my job for nothing, pick up her bag and fly back to the emergency door that gave out behind the back seats. She had it open in a second and was out into the blackness and I thought she was running.

The Cypriot driver turned a face that was frantic with alarm. He was only a young chap, and good-looking like most young Cypriots. He shouted something in Greek, and then he grabbed for his door and shouted in English: 'Get out — quick! We're over the edge of the precipice!'

He hardly needed to tell us that last bit of information. That jarring and this angle at which the bus now rested told the story just as well.

Panic set in. More than a dozen passengers began a frantic scramble out through the doors and windows into the night outside. The women were screaming. The men weren't thinking of manly dignity and were bawling in fear and shoving their way out heedless of who stood before them.

I went out through a window. That was easy for me. When I was on the trail I looked back into that lighted bus and saw the fat, frightened features of my ex-boss. B.G. wasn't built for getting through windows, and every time he tried to get out of his seat the throng of stampeding folk shoved him back. He was bleating something in his fear. He reckoned he was going down that precipice alone in that bus any second now.

It turned out that none of our fears was justified. That bus was balanced precariously with one wheel overhanging the edge of that chasm — a chasm we couldn't see because of the darkness — but it seemed firm enough while the brakes were on. But we didn't think of that until we were all out on that mountain trail, B.G. included.

He was fluttering like an old hen. He came searching for me quickly, and when he found me he grabbed me and held on to me like a child to his mom. That's the part of my job — the job I'd just lost — that I didn't like. I was supposed to be the trouble-buster for the Gissenheim Corporation. Whenever they ran into trouble in their overseas projects, I was the man drafted in to sort things out.

But I was also wet nurse to the boss, B.G. He was a timid man, for all his imposing appearance and bulk, and he was terrified to be alone in foreign cities. So I had to tag along to keep him company and bolster up his confidence.

Now it needed some bolstering. But so did mine.

The whole crowd of us stood within the yellow lights of that stranded bus on that steep-sloping trail, and a lot of us trembled, and all of us made remarks such as: 'For crying out loud!' And —

'Cripes, I thought we were over that time!'

Come to think of it, both those remarks were mine. All other remarks at first seemed to be in Greek, Turkish or some other Cypriot language. I did realise that a feminine, fluttery voice was saying something in almost hysterical English. That would be one of the two skinny, spinster-like types that had sat in front of us.

Then that Cypriot driver jumped out of his agitation and remembered that bub back along the trail. He shouted something in violent anger in Greek, and then he must have seen the two Americans standing by him for he translated: 'That fellow. He did it. He made me swing out.' A flow of Greek and then: 'I don't know what happened. I thought he was falling under our wheels.'

I started to move back up the trail. I had a torch. The Cypriot driver came walking up with me. I could feel him bristling with anger. When he got hold of that fellow he was going to do an awful lot of bad things to him.

But someone had done them before us. My light probed along the roadway. The approaching storm helped with a sudden flash of lightning and the whole mountainside was illuminated, and we saw that body lying only a few yards ahead of us across the road.

The Cypriot was exclaiming: 'I didn't hit him! He started to fall before we were near him. But I didn't hit him.' He was still saying that when I knelt beside that man in the roadway.

A violent gust of wind came tearing up from the sea just then. It seemed solid and wet and warm. I thought: We'd better hurry. That storm will be upon us in a few minutes.

I turned the body over. For it was a body. The man was dead. I knew that before I put my hand on him.

What I was interested in was — how had he come by his death?

My torch shone on his face. I heard the Cypriot driver, kneeling besides me now, gasp. I knew he'd recognised that round face with its heavy blue jowl. The eyes were partly open and I saw the whites and they made him look somehow blind.

That Cypriot driver was saying things under his breath, and there was almost awe in his voice. Clearly he was surprised to the point of being shocked by recognition, and I wanted to ask him who this dead man was and why he'd produced such an effect on our Cypriot driver. But for the moment this wasn't the time.

My torch bathed in brilliant white light the open-necked shirt of the dead man. It was an expensive shirt. This was no poor wandering peasant of a man.

But I didn't dwell long on the quality of his shirt. What made my eyes widen was the suffusing blood just over the man's heart. It had stained his shirt, and even as we watched, the stain, black in that light, was spreading.

I pulled on that shirt and lifted it and shone my torch close to it at the same time. I'd got a hunch. The hunch was right.

There was a neat hole drilled through that cloth. I knew if I looked on to the man's chest I would find a similar neat hole drilling right through the body just where the heart was.

I was looking in amazement at that corpse, when I saw feet and pants come just to the edge of the circle of light thrown by my torch. The other passengers were coming up.

Then all at once a succession of thoughts impacted upon me. I came lurching to my feet. My eyes went round into the blackness about us. I was thinking: Someone shot this poor bub just as he was trying to stop the bus. The killer must be lurking somewhere around in this blackness.

That set me off walking towards the crowd down by the yellow lights of that bus. The Cypriot was walking by my side. That other passenger was crowding up behind us. I said to the driver: 'He got shot. You never touched him.'

The driver had seen that wound but he hadn't thought of death by a gunshot wound. Those thoughts don't occur to people easily in the normal way of life.

He exclaimed excitedly: 'I knew I

didn't run on to him.' His pride in his driving ability was at stake and he was quick to prove himself in the clear. And then he added: 'He was shot . . . ' He said it thoughtfully, as if he was casting his mind back.

We were coming down towards the bus, but still away from its lights.

I heard the Cypriot begin to say: 'Look, I saw something in my mirror. Just when Christopholou began to fall. I saw — '

No one ever knew what that Cypriot driver saw. There was a flurry of movement behind me. I went down on my knees as weight crashed out of the darkness into my back. My torch bounced and went swinging into space, its beam bracketing as it plummeted into the void.

Then that Cypriot driver was following after the torch. He was over the edge, carried over by that sudden, treacherous rush. Rolling on to my side in a quick getup, I heard his scream of mortal fear, and it lasted a long, long time, trailing away into distance as he fell. Then there was silence.

I just stood and listened and couldn't move until there was nothing more to be heard of that Cypriot driver who had gone over the edge. Then, when he was silent far below, I came whirling round.

The killer had struck again from the darkness. He had thrown that Cypriot into the void at a moment when the driver was about to say something to me of seeming importance concerning the death of this lone wayfarer on the trail.

I was crouching, my fists balled defensively, waiting for another attack from that deadly blackness — this time an attack upon me, Joe P. Heggy.

None came.

The crowd by the bus was silent. They didn't understand that dying scream of the Cypriot driver. All they knew was that awful things were happening in this terrifying darkness around them.

Forked lightning split the heavens only a few miles north of us. The roll of thunder out at sea was almost continuous. Again that mighty, pressing wind came reaching up at us from the coastal plain, seeming to try to drive us over that precipice also.

I went battling head down against the blast. A few raindrops pattered on me. I knew within minutes the storm would break, and I'd had experience of storms in Cyprus before. It wasn't going to be fun, stuck on this road high in the mountains during a thunderstorm.

Yet I only gave half my mind to the storm. What I was more concerned about was this killer in the darkness — the killer who had disposed of — what was his name? Christopholou? — and then ditched the poor Cypriot when he'd seemed about to say something important.

I tried in those few seconds before I reached the bus to think what the driver had been saying. Something about his mirror. I didn't understand.

Then I thought of the name, Christopholou. I knew I'd heard it somewhere recently, but I couldn't place it then. At that moment I couldn't place much in my mind at all, because I was too busy watching the lightning-riven blackness for the killer, and that seemed a worthwhile, full-time occupation then.

It was raining fairly heavily, big drops slanting almost horizontally at us, impelled by the weight of that mighty, roaring wind. The crowd had gathered behind the bus, to seek protection from that blast. They all started to talk as I came up.

I saw the bus lights reflecting on the prissy octagonal-edged glasses of big, heavy B.G. His fat face looked bewildered and terrified. He liked to pose as a big, ruthless tycoon, but we employees of the Gissenheim Corporation knew him to be as craven as a chicken at heart.

I thought I'd scare him out of his pants. I said: 'There's murder on the road. This road.'

Faces lifted to peer at me, fascinated and aghast. I caught the flash of eyes as they tried to see into mine. About a dozen of them there'd be, crouching in the lee of that bus. A dozen. I started to look again, trying to identify them. I was looking for someone.

Someone was missing.

A small round apple of a man shoved himself forward importantly. He said: 'Look, I'm taking charge. I'm a detective

— a private investigator.' It was very dark, but I could feel him swelling up with pride as he said it. 'You'll have heard of me. My name's Girais Keremetlian.'

I said to him, grimly: 'Brother, you can take charge. I don't see what there is you can take charge of, but — you take charge.'

They began to talk then in many languages, but all were questions I knew. I tried to explain, briefly.

'There's a fellow lying across the road back there. The one our driver swerved to avoid. He's dead. I never saw a man more dead.'

That apple of a man with the Armenian sounding name said quickly: 'How did he die?'

'Someone put a bullet through his heart.' I looked into those towering hills around us, just pile upon pile of rock from which grew an occasional shrub or tree. The lightning faded and there was darkness, and I thought of all the killers who could be in those rocks watching us now.

There was a gasp of horror at my

words. I was looking at the Armenian. His fat, cheerful face was sagging suddenly. I kept my eyes on him carefully as I said: 'Then the killer came out of the darkness and threw our Cypriot driver over the edge.' I jerked my head significantly towards the big drop.

They seemed to melt into one fused group at that. They came closer together, as if seeking mutual protection. I never saw such a frightened huddle in my life. And that cocky little Armenian was trying frantically to get into the middle of the huddle, like a pup trying to get to the centre of the pack for warmth and protection.

I called: 'Hey, you, I thought you were taking charge of this case. You're a 'tec, aren't you?'

He didn't come out from the huddle. Shamelessly he exclaimed: 'I'm off the case. I just took myself off. Two murders — that's not in my line!'

It wasn't in my line, either. I stood there, wondering what to do. I had my back to the bus now, and I was watching into the darkness, my eyes searching quickly whenever the lightning crackled and lit up the streaming, wet hillside. I never saw a thing, but I knew the killer must be near to us.

I remembered those feet and pants legs that had come within the orbit of my torch when I was examining Christopholou. I wondered which of the passengers they belonged to.

The wind was blowing up again and the rain was cascading down. I shouted: 'Which one of you came after me up the road with the driver?'

No one answered. I felt a chill creep down my spine. I was thinking: I was standing there within inches of the murderer. I never knew it. It was the murderer who sent me flying and then tipped that poor Cypriot over the edge.

I lost weight, sweating at the thought. I kept on losing weight because of the menace of this stormy darkness here in the mountains. And I was wet through, I suddenly realised, because it was raining heavily and I hadn't been noticing it.

I looked at the people, huddling in the lee of that bus. They were all getting wet.

The storm was moving overhead now, and the rain was bouncing up a foot high from the wet roadway that was rapidly becoming a watercourse.

I shouted: 'We can't stay here all night.' But there was nowhere for people to find shelter on that inhospitable mountainside. Nowhere that I could see, anyway.

I fought my way against the storm blast to that rear door out of which that lovely Greek girl had plunged the moment we'd halted over the edge of the chasm. I pulled myself into the coach. And then I turned.

'I don't know about you, but I'm going to sit inside during the storm.'

I saw big Berny, his face streaming with rain, as he looked from the darkness at the warm light still glowing inside that bus. His lips said something but I didn't hear them because the wind whipped away all sound. I guessed, though.

I leaned out of the door, shouting down to those huddled folk: 'I reckon the bus is safe enough. If we all sit at the back we won't go toppling into the valley.'

Even so, they didn't come in immediately at that. It seemed suicide to get into that bus where it lay overhanging the edge of the precipice. Then the rain came down almost solidly, and that settled the matter. They almost fought to get under that roof upon which the rain drummed so loudly it was impossible to hear yourself speak. I sat to one side and watched them come in. I wanted to see if that Greek girl had come back.

She hadn't. She didn't come in with the passengers anyway.

I lit a cigarette and stared out into the darkness. I was wondering what had happened to her. Wondering where she was now in this storm. I wondered if she had run over the edge of the precipice herself in her panic, and it made me swallow because she was too young and too lovely to meet with such a brutal fate.

And I wondered who she was.

My eyes suddenly narrowed. I was remembering that, only seconds before we'd seen that figure standing in the road, she had been buttoning her light, summer coat and positioning her handbag on her knees in the manner of a person about to rise and depart. I remembered all that, suddenly, curiously.

She certainly had departed in a hurry. She'd been the first out and that was, I suddenly realised, because she'd been intending to get up out of her seat around about that time, anyway.

I watched the smoke ascend in the yellow light of that sloping bus. We pulled blinds down to keep the rain out, because this bus didn't have glass in its windows. They don't, not in summer in Cyprus.

I had a sudden thought: 'But these blinds won't keep bullets out.'

I still couldn't forget that the killer had been out there in the darkness, and for all I knew the killer was out there right now.

Then I thought: 'Someone's got to go up to that body and do something about it.' Because you don't leave a body lying in the roadway in the middle of a storm. It somehow doesn't seem fitting and proper.

I knew I was the one who would have to go out and attend to the late Mr. Christopholou.

2

There was a girl...

I got to my feet. We were all sitting in those rear seats of the sloping bus. I saw faces lift towards mine when I got on to my feet. They were mostly frightened faces, wet and bedraggled from those minutes out there in the storm. I saw fear in those eyes — and suspicion. As if they thought I might have had something to do with those killings myself.

It was an eerie, grotesque situation I found myself in at that moment. I seemed to be in a world of silence — a silence between human beings, at any rate — because of that wind that came roaring through the windowless apertures on our coach, and because of that frenzied pounding of driving rain upon the roof of our vehicle.

The wind drove the rain in, so that the passengers now crouched between the seats to get protection. They looked tawdry, unlovely, painfully cold.

It was hard to think that only a little while before we had found the heat of the night almost insupportable. Now there were red noses and blanched cheeks, and teeth were probably chattering but they passed unheard in that violent storm.

Berny's unhappy face looked up at me from where he too crouched between two seats. I saw his lips frame an anxious: 'Where are you going?'

I shouted: 'Back there.' My head jerked towards where the body was lying exposed to this storm. I framed words with my lips so that he could understand. 'I reckon I've got to put Christopholou where he won't come to any more harm.' I was thinking that maybe this floodwater on the road might be sufficient to wash him over the edge after the bus driver. The police wouldn't want that to happen.

They must all have been watching me in the yellow light of those dimming lamps. The batteries were running down fast. They must have read those words, as well as that shambling hulk of a boss of mine, shivering in his expensive New York summer suiting.

Especially they must have got that name, Christopholou. I saw mouths suddenly frame O's of excitement. And eyes were wide and incredulous.

There were four or five people only whose faces didn't register — lean-faced, swarthy Cypriot types who wore the black, baggy-seated trousers and calf-high leather boots of the country dweller. And lean-faced, swarthy womenfolk, their kind.

But there was also that big, going-soft young woman with a man who was probably her father or grandfather. A sullen, unpleasant-eyed little man who watched her all the time as if expecting her to behave in a manner improper to Cypriot maidens.

She'd tried, too, coming up. She'd kept looking across in interested fashion at the Americans, B.G. and me.

There had been a lot of green light in those cow-like brown eyes of hers, but she was too naïve, too unsophisticated in her technique. We'd let the green light ride.

In any event my attention was directed towards that other Greek-Cypriot — the slim, ultra-sophisticated girl who had ducked out of the bus and was now lost in the storm.

There was the Armenian dick, shivering and looking as unhappy as any of them now. And a thin man with glasses whose face seemed unnaturally white about the pointed chin. A man who seemed to be detached from his present surroundings even now; he seemed somehow remote behind his glasses, like a man lost in thought. I put him down as a Britisher. I don't know why, but he had that look.

There was a big, heavy-bellied man, who looked massively prosperous. He was looking at me with surprise even greater than anyone else's on his big round face. I saw him repeat back to me, though I never heard a sound — 'Christopholou?'

I shrugged. I didn't know what the excitement was about. But even so I kept thinking with part of my mind: Now, where have I heard that name before?

It wasn't a usual name. If I'd heard it in

some context I should have remembered it. But I didn't.

I got the rear door open. As I descended once more into the driving wetness of that road I looked at those coach lights and I thought: They won't last more than half an hour or so.

Then I went floundering back up the road. The wind tried to throw me on my face. The rain soaked me through to the skin. But then I was wearing, like B.G., a lightweight summer suiting. I hadn't brought any coat along with me. I didn't expect to need it in August in Cyprus.

It was only when I'd gone into that darkness of the stormbound mountain track that I realised this time I was without a torch. I hesitated. I tried to tell myself that it wasn't any good going on without a torch. I might walk over the edge in the dark, and that wouldn't help the police tomorrow.

But I found I couldn't go back. Somehow it seemed wrong to sit in the comparative comfort of that coach and leave a recently murdered man to be washed by the rains of the night. I found myself going cautiously up the road.

Water was running down several inches deep. Small stones were coming with it. It wasn't pleasant, and I was walking bent almost double, my fingers reaching forward and touching the roadway ahead — a roadway I could no longer see.

I went with tremendous care. At this point the road was straight, I remembered, and I thought I could keep to it and not go over the edge. But I still took elaborate care to keep my neck intact.

I found the corpse. The water was running so hard against it that I felt it pooled up on the far side of the body. I guessed that the weight of the water was gradually rolling the corpse down the steep-sloping roadway.

I knelt beside it for a second, gasping as the cold, driving rain lashed through my thin clothes. I could see one evidence only of human life in this dark world. The lights of the coach. And even they were sometimes obscured for seconds on end when a particularly violent deluge was hurled by that monstrous, all-engulfing wind.

There was no other sign of life. Nothing to see.

I turned to that body and took it under the arms and began to drag it down the hill against the storm. It was hard work. I had to fight all the way against that wind, and the deceased was no lightweight. Gasping, I dragged the body up to the rear of the coach. It wasn't any good putting it inside the bus, because those people couldn't have stood it, I guess.

So I rolled it under the rear of the vehicle, wedging it against one of the double-tyred wheels.

I figured it would stay there the night and not come to any great harm. I wasn't so sure about the rest of us.

Then I got back into the coach and everyone looked at me either as a hero or as the murderer himself. It took me a few seconds to work out their reactions.

Then I realised that some were fully convinced that the darkness outside was peopled by a waiting, menacing, bunch of killers. To have gone and retrieved that corpse under those circumstances was heroic to the protagonists of this theory.

But in the surly, suspicious eyes of others I could only have braved the storm and any other dangers because I was the killer myself. I looked around at those faces sardonically. I could read their thoughts. It didn't worry me.

There were other things that worried me. One was this damned bus in which we sat. The wind was getting more and more violent, and now the coach was rocking under the fierce blast. It wasn't nice to think that one wheel of our bus was already dangling in mid-air over the edge of a precipice. I remembered those stones that were being washed down the roadway, and I thought that maybe more might be washed off the edge of this precipice.

I looked down that steep sloping coach, cocked at this unnatural attitude, and I thought: This old bus is going to take a nosedive before morning.

But I didn't move. It was illogical, but it felt better sitting inside this rocking coffin than being exposed on that dark trail in the full fury of the night's storm. And that, I reckon, is how the others were thinking about it.

We just sat there for maybe twenty minutes or so while the storm raged directly overhead. The blinds were being ripped to ribbons and made useless. Now if we lifted our heads we could see out through the open windows all around us. We could see nothing.

But I don't suppose I was the only one there who thought: The killer out there can see us every time we move!

We all felt that the killer was still lurking in the vicinity. We all remembered that he had a gun and could use it. We kept imagining that he was somewhere clinging to the rocky hillside across the trail from us, looking in on us as we crouched between the seats of that bus.

I looked across and saw some of the Cypriot women. I knew they were moaning, and their eyes were rolling in frantic terror.

Then that handsome, soft-looking Cypriot, with her rather fat fingers in heavy rings, started to have hysterics, wedged between two seats by that elderly man who was accompanying her.

I could feel them cracking. They couldn't stand this strain much longer. I felt that I couldn't stand it much longer, either.

There came a moment when it seemed as if the storm became intensified beyond anything I had ever known before. Almost it seemed as if the rain would smash right through the roof of this old bus, and it was blowing in through the windows so that we were wetted again as we crouched for protection behind the seats. Water was running all over the floor of the bus. The lights dimmed again.

Then that big portly Greek Cypriot with the heavy blue jowl seemed to lose his nerve. That was curious. I would have thought maybe one of those thin English women would have cracked up first. Or those excitable Cypriots. But it was the biggest man among us who lost his head.

The bus was swaying again under the violence of the wind, and he let out a yell that even we heard above the drumming noise upon the roof of the bus. He jumped for the door and opened it and went out into the blackness.

I stayed where I was. I couldn't think what good it would do to go out there into the dark . . .

And then, miraculously, the storm abated for a few moments. All at once the wind seemed to blow away and we were left in a calm. The rain almost ceased, and after the frantic hammering above our heads the silence seemed immense . . . silence, though everywhere around us lightning danced and crackled above the high-peaked mountains.

We began to stir and sit up. We were cramped and cold and shivering and wanted movement to get the blood circulating in our limbs again.

The lights seemed suddenly to go much dimmer.

The Cypriots across the way from me were talking excitedly and in great fear. They were terrified of this bus they were in. The English women began to push back bedraggled hair and make themselves look more presentable. But their eyes were filled with fear, too.

Only that thin man with glasses, that Englishman as I supposed, sat huddled into the corner of the back seat and didn't indicate his thoughts by any change of expression.

Berny came crawling round to me. His teeth were chattering and his face looked fatter than ever. He moaned: 'Do something, Heggy. You got me into this, now get me out.'

I snarled: 'I don't work for you any more. You fired me back down the road. Get yourself out.'

I was as uncomfortable and miserable as Berny, and I didn't see why I should put up with his griping. Anyway, the reason why I was on this bus had gone . . . that dame who looked like a Greek goddess.

Berny blinked at me and used a wet handkerchief to try to rub the rain out of his hair. It wasn't particularly successful. He was so uncomfortable that he snarled back at me, and that was a thing he rarely did. 'It's dames, Heggy. That's your trouble. They get you into holes like this.' He blinked rapidly in that failing light, a fat man filled with indignation. 'And your dames get me into trouble, too.'

I stood up. I told him to quit yapping. And yet I knew it was true.

We'd come by morning plane into Cyprus. We'd travelled down from the airfield to Nicosia, principal city of Cyprus. We were on our way out to a northern tourist resort called Kyrenia and the plan had been to get a hired car to take us over the mountains to the coast.

But during lunch in an hotel I'd registered with a girl who looked like everything you've ever read about Greek goddesses.

She was tall and stately and she had everything in the right places and a face to match. She was made for Joe P. Heggy — though I seem to remember that thought coming into the Heggy mind many times in the past adult years.

Let me say right off that I knew her type. She looked like a goddess, but I wasn't kidded. She was too self-contained, too bold in the way she gazed around and looked at a man, to be any goddess. And when she looked at me, an obvious American, there had been warm light in her eyes, an invitation a yard long.

She'd been around, that girl. But so had I. And it seemed to me we might go around together, at least for the time that I was on the island.

We progressed pretty well from a distance in that hotel restaurant. I knew she was willing to play. B.G., my boss, knew what I was up to and he was getting all shocked and virtuous. I took no heed of him. You don't take much heed of bosses nowadays.

All I knew was he'd brought me to this island, and I intended to make the most of it. That dark, glossy-haired Greek girl was made for leisure.

That dark, glossy-haired girl suddenly switched off the charm and all in one second it seemed that I didn't exist. It seemed to me that suddenly she became apprehensive, panicky, I saw her rise in haste and go to a telephone booth within the hotel lobby. She wasn't there long. When she came out she hurried into the brilliant sunshine and went across to where the long-distance buses were parked.

I was startled. I don't like dames

walking out on me in that manner. I'd been planning a brilliant future. Now there was no future.

Then I saw the sign on the bus she got on to. It said Kyrenia . . . that was the place we were heading for.

B.G. found himself being hoisted to his feet. He was blinking and bewildered. I was suddenly arguing that not even a millionaire could afford to hire cars to take him thirty or forty or however many miles it was to Kyrenia.

I started to enthuse about travelling the way the locals travelled, that that way a tourist came into contact with the people and was able to see and observe and enjoy accordingly.

I wasn't quite sure what you could see and observe and enjoy, but I piled it on good and thick. B.G found himself being bustled out and across that square to where the old bus throbbed and shook as its engine warmed up.

He yelped that he didn't want to travel by uncomfortable bus. Godammit, didn't he have enough money to buy a whole fleet of buses?

I told him not to be a snob. Because I knew that was why B.G. didn't want to be seen in a bus. B.G. liked to pose as a big shot always, and big shots couldn't be seen in ordinary public conveyances. He was for a private car to take him out to the coast in style. I was for a bus.

I won.

B.G. fired me less than ten miles out of Kyrenia. All the time he'd griped about the dust from the roads and the unsprung seats and the general discomfort of that lurching, noisy, fume-stinking bus.

I got tired of him after a time. I wanted to concentrate on that Greek girl, but she didn't look at me all that journey. She was a changed woman. I didn't like the change.

Joe P. Heggy doesn't like the cold-shoulder from any female. So I got bad-tempered and in one word I reflected considerably on my boss's ancestry.

B.G. objected to being called names by an employee. He squealed I was fired and could look for another job. I grunted back: 'The hell, I never did think much of the job, anyway. Playing nursemaid to a big fat slob like you!'

I got all those thoughts into my mind in those seconds while I sat on that wet seat, and I wished I hadn't been a dumb-cluck and I thought how nice a private car would have been. At least it would have had windows, and it wouldn't have run us into murder.

B.G. was scared stiff. He wasn't sitting upright but was bent forward by my side, looking up at me furtively.

I realised that the others weren't sitting bolt upright either. Then I realised what it was.

They had substituted one nerve-breaking fear for another. The storm that had threatened to throw them over the precipice was gone for the moment. Now they remembered that a killer was loose in the vicinity — a cold-blooded killer who had killed twice within a few minutes.

I began to get prickles on my skull, too. And shivers coursed down my spine. I found myself staring through that window to where our yellow lights reflected feebly upon the wet surfaces of the rocky mountainside that bordered this road.

I began to feel jumpy again. I kept imagining I saw movement. My mouth went dry as I thought: We're sitting birds for that guy with his gun out there in the dark.

It was so bad, sitting there inside that lighted bus and feeling that eyes were watching, that I couldn't stand it any longer. I growled to B.G.: 'Move your fat carcass. I'm going out.'

I went out. I wondered where the big, heavy Greek-Cypriot had got to. I didn't have long to wait to find out.

He was crouching under the rear of the bus. I saw movement and guessed it was he. I thought: You wouldn't stay there, brother, if you knew there was a corpse tucked against the other tyre.

I called him out. He stood up, probably ashamed, but I couldn't see his face in that dark. He was shaking so violently either with cold or fear that I could feel the trembling of his bulk in the darkness.

I told him to get inside the bus. It might be a bit warmer there. He went in and I saw the door shut. I thought I heard a sound simultaneously in the darkness and came wheeling round, my fists up and ready. I put my back against the bus.

But there was no movement within the circle of feeble light that came from the bus. I guessed probably some stone had come rolling down the hillside on to the road. But I stood there a long time. I was thinking of many things, and especially of that Greek girl.

I was wondering why she had changed so abruptly towards me. Why there had seemed to be panic on her lovely, patrician face. I wondered where she had got to in this blinding darkness.

I didn't want to stay there, because I could see more rain beating up. The lightning was still playing about those rugged hills and I guessed we were in for another cloudburst any minute.

But I didn't want to go back inside that bus. I thought, if I go back in there I'll get the heeby-jeebies. All those people inside that bus were filled with terror. Fear is contagious. I'd be a jittery wreck myself in no time, I knew.

I thought: I'm going to risk a walk down the road. Maybe I'll see something.

I wasn't optimistic. They didn't build houses in isolated parts such as these — not usually, anyway. Still, I could only try.

I got up the back way through the emergency door again. The lights were very dim now. That was another reason why I should move if I was going to move at all that night. I told them what I was going to do and they all looked at me with faces filled with concern and terror. I knew they were thinking: He'll never come back.

I tried to look nonchalant. I didn't feel so good, all the same. I didn't like all that blackness outside, and the thought of that chasm off the roadway gave me the willies. And every now and then I remembered that killer who had shot one man and thrown another to his death over a precipice.

But I couldn't stay there. I felt I had to take advantage of this lull in the storm and try to find help for us.

41

There was just one thing I wanted to know before I left that bus.

In the doorway, I asked: 'Look, who was Christopholou?'

There was a silence. I call it a bad silence. They were all looking at me as if I shouldn't have asked that question.

And then one of those thin, vein-mottled-faced Englishwomen answered me. She said: 'Christopholou was the man who got away. His companion, Yangos Joanou, was executed.'

I walked away from that bus remembering the details.

There was an anarchistic movement on this island. To put it more bluntly, there were people who had watched events in Palestine, and now in Kenya, and they'd decided that the best way to get rid of the British in Cyprus was to start bumping off some of the top fellows. They had made an attempt on the Governor. It had been unsuccessful, but someone had died in the crowd as the result of the attempted assassination.

As I faced the blackness of that night I remembered what I had read in the papers about the affair. The anarchists had got away. Then somehow the authorities had got the name of one of them — Yangos Joanou — and he'd been hauled in, tried and hanged.

I tried to think what was curious about the affair. Something to do with the way Joanou had been found . . .

Then I stopped thinking about Christopholou, the man who had got away, only to die by a bullet himself. The storm was beating up and I was finding my way now by the almost non-stop lightning that flashed across the northern sky. The rain was coming down harder.

But the storm still wasn't on me, and in that I was fortunate. For I hadn't gone more than a few hundred yards round the first bend in the road when I saw a light ahead of me. If the rain had been coming down as it had previously I wouldn't have seen that light.

I went plunging recklessly towards it. After a while, with the rain coming down harder than ever, I realised that I had to climb off the roadway to get to it. It was a lonely villa, set back off the road.

I followed a short pathway, pausing when the lightning faded, and moving quickly forward when it came to illuminate that wet landscape. I think I shouted as I came up towards the villa, but a roll of thunder must have drowned the sound of my voice.

I went straight towards that light. It was coming from a long, French window. The curtains were apart, so that as I stumbled in my water-filled boots towards it I could see straight into that room.

There was a girl inside towelling her hair. She was wearing a long, leaf-green nylon robe. When I saw her, even before I saw her face, I guessed who it was.

That Greek girl with the panic in her eyes who had rushed from the bus the moment it had halted back up the road a way.

3

Something is wrong

I stumbled on to a porch. That's how we'd call it, anyway. I was under cover, and I could look in through that window, and the girl didn't know I was there.

For some reason I didn't knock on the door immediately. And it wasn't just that I wanted to get an eyeful of that pliant young form there, so clearly revealed with each movement of her uplifted arms as she towelled the moisture out of her hair. I was trying to put things together. I knew there was something deep about all this, something that connected and ran on. And it started, I felt, with that short telephone call the girl had put through in Nicosia.

I thought: She was getting ready to alight from the bus. Maybe the bus driver knew to put her down at this bend.

I thought of Christopholou, the man

45

who had been murdered. I thought maybe she had phoned him from Nicosia, and maybe he had been on the road to meet her.

I thought maybe she had asked him to meet her because of whatever had made her panic.

Christopholou . . . A man wanted by the police of Cyprus for his part in an attempted assassination. This gal didn't pick good company.

She didn't. Next moment she had me for company.

I didn't knock. I walked straight in. She dropped the towel from her face as the storm rushed in with me. I've never seen anyone look so suddenly scared in all my life.

And then she saw me, a highly-drenched Heggy, and relief flooded back to her face in a way that was noticeable even to a man as unnoticing as I am.

I knew that for one split second she had thought it might be someone else . . .

For a second or two I could only stand there and gasp and try to get my breath back. Then I climbed out of my suit coat.

It wasn't doing me any good, as full of rainwater as it was. I reached out. I said: 'Babe, I could do with a towel, too.'

Then the storm hit us again. The lull was over. The wind screamed as it tore at that villa, and I thought of it tearing at that stranded bus and trying to rock it over the edge into that great, yawning chasm, terrifyingly there even though it was unseen.

Mechanically she handed that towel to me. Her hair was in disorder, all black and frizzed up where her towelling had disarranged it. She was without shoes, and it made her look shorter than I'd remembered her. And my guess was that there was nothing under that wrap but her own fine figure. She looked somehow rather dumpy and round — but when I say dumpy I don't mean she was any the less attractive for it.

This gal had everything, even for a man whose teeth were chattering with cold after a fight in a cold night storm.

I heard her say: 'The others? Did anyone come with you?'

I got the water out of my ears. 'Nope. I

came on alone. The others are drowning in the bus right now, I reckon. Or maybe they've got blown over the precipice.'

She turned away. I looked round quickly. This was a summer retreat for some wealthy person, obviously.

It was simply furnished, but there was a suggestion of luxury about it. It looked good to me. I noticed for the first time that the light came from a petrol burner. There'd be no telephone, I knew without looking.

She was turning her head to watch me again, and her face was trying to register pleasure. I said: 'You got off the mark mighty quick, lady. I never saw anyone get out of a bus so quickly.'

She didn't say anything. Not with her tongue. But she was giving me her eyes, and they were big and brown, and there was plenty to give. I got it that she had decided she needed me as a friend and ally. I was prepared to be a friend and ally of those big, brown eyes any day.

But there were things I wanted to know. I said: 'How come you found this place so easily?'

'I just ran.' She had a deep voice, one of those voices that vibrate with a kind of deep huskiness.

'I thought maybe this was where you'd intended to alight.' I was looking at a picture on a table.

For some reason she lied. It was silly of her. Maybe she didn't know what she was going to gain by telling the truth, and so she risked a whopper. 'Me?' Her eyes widened with innocence. 'No. I didn't know this house was here. I just ran, I told you, until I came upon it.'

I peeled off my shirt. I guessed I'd find another in the house. If not, a blanket would do. 'Why did you run?'

'When I saw Chris — ' She checked herself. 'When I saw that man die back on the road there, I think I panicked. All I knew was that I wanted to get out of that bus and run.'

'You sure ran fast,' I repeated mechanically.

Then I went across to that photograph. It was a picture of that Greek girl, I said: 'I guess you made a mistake, didn't you? I mean, when you said you ran into this

49

place by accident.' I turned the picture towards her.

She knew I'd caught her out. She was shameless. She smiled ravishingly; and she sure was fetching in that get-up. She was putting her hair back in big waves. 'Did I say that? My English, it is not so good. I say things, perhaps, that I do not mean.'

Until that moment her English had been better than mine. I wasn't to be kidded. But I let it pass. I also knew that she knew Christopholou. She'd let that bit slip, too.

I said: 'Have you got an oilskin or mackintosh in the house, honey? I guess I'd better go back to that bus and bring 'em all in. Oh, and a torch, if you've got one.'

Her eyes went hard. She dropped her long eyelashes over them immediately, but I got that change of expression. She didn't speak. Then she came to me as I stood there, towelling my manly Heggy chest. She put her hands on my bare arms and began to stroke me.

I heard her say, as softly as that storm

would let her: 'They'll be all right. Why bother to fetch them in?' Those long lashes lifted for a second to look at me, and then they dropped while she murmured: 'This is a small place. It is just big enough for . . . two.'

She had a pretty direct technique. Sometimes I would have gone for it. I could almost have gone for it there, because those wraps don't wrap all the way.

I said: 'Give me that routine some other time, baby, and you'll see a different Heggy. Right now, though, I can't play footsie-wootsie with you while those poor devils go clean out of their minds, or suffer even worse.'

Her eyes snapped at me then. She was a woman scorned. Or she could add it up to mean that if she wanted. But there was something more than just outraged pride behind that look. I got it again — fear.

That dame didn't want those passengers in the same house with her. I began to understand now why she'd legged it from that bus in such a hell of a hurry.

I was walking around that pleasant,

barely-furnished room. I was looking for the name Christopholou somewhere, because I was sure this was his cottage, and this was where he had been hiding out from the authorities. I didn't see anything to help that theory, and so I turned and said quickly to the girl: 'Christopholou must have found it pleasant — here with you.'

I saw the leaping light come into those big, brown eyes at the mention of the name. She said, quickly: 'Christopholou? You know him?'

I nodded back up the roadway. 'We got introduced. A bullet did it. Now he's lying under a bus, pretty dead.'

That could have been a brutal thing to say to a girl who has been living with a man, but I knew it wasn't going to hurt her.

It didn't hurt her. She turned away, and her long, red-taloned fingernails probed in a box for a cigarette. She was thinking. I knew her kind. She was wondering how all this affected her.

She lit up and looked at me through the smoke. 'I thought he was dead,' she said softly. Then it was her turn to ask a question. She did it boldly. 'You know Christopholou?'

I'd found a shirt in a set of drawers. I reckoned Christopholou wouldn't mind and I put it on.

'They told me about him back at the bus.' I remembered the expressions on those faces when that English spinster dame came up with the identity. They'd been — frightened.

'Christopholou was quite a boy, wasn't he? Ready to bump off anyone he didn't like.'

She retorted coolly, without heat: 'No . . . ready to bump off the British in an effort to get them off this island.'

The way she said it I couldn't figure out whether she approved of the idea or not.

I wasn't hurrying now. That storm outside was pretty violent, and mentally I was shirking going back into it. And that tall Greek girl — because even without her shoes she still rated high, for a woman — that girl looked enough to keep any man hanging around. And Joe P. Heggy is impressionable.

I found a suit coat. It didn't fit me.

Christopholou must have had a lot of fat on his shoulders. But it was dry and warm. The girl was walking about the room now, as if filled with urgent thoughts. And the quicker she paced up and down that polished, uncarpeted floor, the more I saw of her bare, ivory limbs.

When she thought I'd had enough and might be in a more receptive mood, she came back to the attack again. She threw away her cigarette. Her eyes were very big and warm, and holding promise of many things.

She came and stood close up to me again, and again she whispered: 'Don't fetch those people. Just let us stay here together until the storm blows out.'

She put her arms around me then, and I got the perfume of her scented body. Too much perfume. They bath in it, these Mediterranean people. But it had its effect.

I could feel the warmth of her body under that robe, as she pressed against me. And that scent talked as it climbed into my nostrils and befuddled my brain.

I wanted to stay. Don't kid yourself. Few men who are young and with rich red blood coursing through their veins can walk away from a first-class woman who's offering herself.

But I pushed her away. The villa was rocking under a fresh blast of storm-wind. I thought of the terror of those people down at the bus, and I knew that I had to go and try to help them. I found a black oilskin that came nearly to my ankles. It would do. There was a hat, too, and then I found a torch.

The girl was furious. But with her anger was panic again, I could tell. She was following me all the time now, asking me to stay, but especially beginning to say now: 'Don't bring those people in here!'

I had tumbled to it. I said: 'There's someone among those passengers you fear?'

She turned away.

I went on: 'Isn't that cock-eyed? Isn't the man you fear some killer out in this storm at this moment?'

She didn't answer, but her fingers were trembling as she reached for another cigarette. I went on: 'That killer who was lying up in the dark waiting for

Christopholou to come down and meet the bus — do you know him?'

I couldn't think it was any law officer. They don't shoot and run. It seemed to me to be a private vendetta.

She didn't answer again, but then I saw her face come round and look at me, and there was contempt in it, and I couldn't understand it.

It stung a little. I found myself wanting to hurt this hard-boiled female who didn't show emotion when her boyfriend was slain.

I asked: 'You weren't married to Christopholou, were you?' She wasn't the type to marry, I was thinking. Then there was suddenly something I wanted to know. I went back to that picture. I was asking: 'What's your name, baby?'

She stood there with her face averted sullenly. She didn't answer. I held that photograph to the light and read the inscription.

It was in Greek, but I guessed it said only: 'With all my love,' because that's the height of originality when photographs are inscribed.

But I could read one word on it. It was Charmain.

'Charmain?' It was a good name for this exotic flower of the Mediterranean. But again that unusual name was having effect on the Heggy brain cells. I was casting my mind back, remembering what I had read in the papers.

Suddenly I looked at that glamorous judy, and I said in triumph: 'Got you! Charmain . . . There was a Charmain figured in that trial of Joanou. His mistress . . .'

She didn't turn, but the way she sucked quickly, almost savagely, on that cigarette, told me I was onto the truth. I was remembering well — too well for this girl's liking.

I looked at her as she stood there, her back to me. Her black hair had been combed and was in good order again. She looked comely and curvacious as she stood there in that leaf-green nylon dressing gown.

I got myself a cigarette, too. I wanted to know just a little more before I went out into that storm.

I said, softly: 'Joanou goes out. You tie up with his friend. That was quick work, honey.' But what did it add up to?

I couldn't help feeling that it did add up to something, and that something was represented by a corpse on a storm-washed mountainside with a bullet through its heart.

I went on talking, because I felt I was near to getting some important clue to the night's tragedies.

'Christopholou and Joanou were two members of a group of anarchists, weren't they? They thought to do an assassination job on the Governor, but they didn't aim straight.' My mind was racing rapidly now. I was remembering what had lain half-forgotten in my brain cells. 'Then they got Joanou. He was tipped off to the authorities, wasn't he?'

I was just remembering how he was tipped off, too.

That girl whirled on me, her nylon wrap swinging with the force of the movement and clinging close to her well-rounded body. Her eyes were flashing viciously.

'Someone did tip him off. A jealous lover!' She stamped her bare foot, remembering. 'It was the editor of a British newspaper in Cyprus. He was a fool.'

I nodded. 'Yeah, he was a fool. I remember now what he did.'

He'd tipped off the police that Yangos Joanou had been one of the assassins who had tried to get the Governor. Then he'd been unable to resist the temptation to write up a scoop story on it.

He'd gone to town on it, too. He'd given the whole mullarkey.

That was all right, but it provided embarrassment when the police picked up Joanou and stood him on trial. Counsel for the defence made a great song about that newspaper story. It had prejudiced the case against his client, he kept arguing.

It certainly was unethical. The British editor had written up that story in such a way that Joanou was as good as hanged before he was caught. Joanou didn't have a chance to work out a defence to satisfy an unprejudiced jury, because on that island no one could remain unprejudiced after reading the newspaper account.

It had ended with Joanou taking the last walk, all the same, and the newspaper editor most unexpectedly finding himself in dock and being sentenced to three months in jail for contempt. I guess that editor was a mighty surprised man.

Charmain wanted to say a lot to me, I could see. Words began to pour from those red lips that were in need of some make-up. She exclaimed hotly: 'That man — that newspaper editor. He did it for me.'

She put scorn on to that last expression. As if it was unthinkable that any newspaper editor should aspire to her favours. I blew smoke and then stubbed out my cigarette and shoved my hand into that oilskin's pockets. There was something inside of them. It felt like a torch.

I was thinking: This gal seems to have changed hands quite a bit. First Joanou. Then Christopholou. Now it seemed that there had been a third lover in the background, and for all her fine scorn I was willing to bet she had led him along.

Now she was working herself up with fear, and I wanted to know something more about it. So I asked: 'Who shot Christopholou?'

She did that half-turning motion again. Kept her face away from me. She shrugged those shapely shoulders under that clinging leaf-green wrap. 'Someone who didn't like him,' she said.

I lifted the Heggy eyebrows. 'You don't say.'

I was thinking that this dame knew more than she was letting out. Maybe if she'd opened up she wouldn't have been in this state of fear and panic. But she wouldn't talk. I got it then that if she had talked she wouldn't have come out of things too well herself — not that she'd come out at all well so far.

I pulled a newspaper from my pocket. It was months old. I saw headlines: ECHO OF NICOSIA SHOOTING — EDITOR STANDS TRIAL.

There was a picture of the editor under the banner. I took a good look at it.

That picture showed a beard. It had curls on it. It was all nice and literary. A show-off of a beard if I've ever seen one.

There was so much beard you couldn't see the face behind it. Just undistinguished eyes and hair ruffled in an arty manner.

Underneath were the words: '*Editor Peter John Haverford, an exclusive picture.*'

With all those whiskers they could keep it exclusive, I thought. My eyes trailed over a few paragraphs. 'Following upon the sentence of Yangos Joanou, now awaiting execution by hanging in Nicosia Jail, comes an echo of the tragedy in which a Nicosia citizen, George Arthur Paterson, lost his life . . . '

I didn't read any more. Charmain was getting nicely worked up. She wasn't the kind to indulge in hysterics, but she wasn't far from them now. I looked at that lovely Greek face and I saw it was working with emotion, and I knew that that emotion was fear.

She was suddenly clinging to me again, talking, and now in her fear she was forgetting her English, and Greek was coming out along with bits of other languages. She sure was in a panic.

I got it that she was doing her damnedest to stop me going and fetching those people into this villa. She kept exclaiming: 'I will die if you do!'

It put me in a fix. I could feel that her fears were genuine. She was terrified, for some reason, of those passengers — or at least of one of the passengers.

That's how I worked it out. I said: 'Maybe. But if I don't fetch those poor devils, they'll maybe all die. You wouldn't want that, would you?'

She looked as if she would. Anything to save her own skin. And saving her own skin seemed to her to mean being left alone here in this villa. Or at least left alone with harmless Joseph P. Heggy.

I pushed her away. I wasn't too gentle about it, either. There was one thing I had to do and I intended doing it and she wasn't going to turn me from what I had in mind. Those people couldn't be left out in that storm any longer.

From the French window I turned and said: 'Who are you afraid of? What's any passenger ever done to you to get you jiving like this?'

She wouldn't say. She just stood there watching me, realising that I wasn't going to be detained any longer and probably doing some frantic thinking instead.

I turned and went out into the storm. Wind hurled itself against me. Rain crashed on to that long oilskin.

Then someone smacked me on the ear and I went down, right within the light from that villa.

As I rolled I had a momentary impression of the girl standing close against the window, looking out. She couldn't have seen much. Maybe she didn't even see anything. For she turned and went quickly into an inner room where I'd found the clothes closet.

I got to my knees. I still had that torch in my hand. I switched on.

Someone started to run away. I just saw movement, and then the shape was swallowed up in the driving rain. I got to my feet. My head was spinning.

Then the storm blast drove away the effects of that blow with a shock of cold rain upon my now bare head. I teetered on my feet a moment irresolutely, undecided what to do.

And then I went down that rocky pathway towards the road, good and mad at the fellow who had massaged my ear for me. It hadn't done him any good. The heck, I wouldn't do him any good if I could catch him!

I stumbled on to the road in all that darkness and with the rain pounding down upon me and with the world filled with the roaring of continuous thunder in the cloud murk overhead. The blue lightning flashes were fairly constant, so that much of the time I could see, though not too far because of the solid wall of rain that was descending.

I was thinking. A curious little thought was in my mind. I didn't understand it. Someone had smacked me on the ear and sent me sprawling and then had run away.

I couldn't reconcile it at all. The only person I could think of wandering about in this storm was a man who had, cold-bloodedly, twice killed that night. It didn't seem to me to be consistent with murder, for the killer to be satisfied merely to thump my ear.

— Or was he just boxing my ear?

That was the curious thought that came into my mind. I went stumbling on but I never saw anyone until I reached the bus. If I'd run against the killer I wouldn't have been able to do much, anyway. For the killer would have a gun and I was unarmed.

I came up to that bus with my lamp held at arm's length sideways. I'd suddenly realised what a target I pre-sented for an unseen gunman when I held the torch in the conventional position immediately in front of my body.

I didn't want to be an easy target, so I held that torch at arm's length and hoped that if anyone took a pot at me they'd miss me by a yard.

They weren't in that bus when I got up to it. But the bus was still there. They'd got so terrified of the lurching of that hulk when the storm blast hit it that they had got down and were all standing to the rear of the vehicle, at least partly protected from that appalling wind.

As I came up, flashing my torch, I saw their wet faces turn towards me. They were all cowering together for warmth and protection. The Armenian private eye was right in the middle among the women. He was a fine tec, I thought.

They couldn't tell who it was advancing with that torch, of course, and there was fear on most of those faces. Then I shouted and they must have got my voice, and B.G. came up from under the coach. He, at any rate, was glad to see me.

I stood there and shouted: 'Follow me! There's a house around the corner!'

Someone translated. Then there was movement. Someone came leaping out towards me. I saw a round face that was suddenly smiling. It was that round, apple-like Armenian, Keremetlian. He was shouting urgently: 'Come on, let's go.'

He was in a helluva hurry. I said: 'Whoa, let's wait for the others, darn you.'

He was an impatient little man, and he got angry with the others, because they were so slow. I saw him bullying them, shrilling at them in their own language. We all began to walk with our heads bent against the driving rain. I led the way, my torch helping when the lightning failed to show us the big drop off the edge of the road. The others crowded on my heels like sheep following a leader.

I got the uncomfortable feeling that we were all sheep, myself included. But that didn't stop me. There was warmth and comfort just around the corner. We'd feel better there.

We got around the corner, buffeted by that shrieking, malicious storm-wind that had come over the sea from nearby Anatolia. Then I found the rocky pathway that led up to the villa, and we began to see occasional light as the rain shifted momentarily. We climbed towards the villa and now our pace was accelerated at the thought of the comfort so near to hand.

I could hear women sobbing with relief behind me, but all the men were curiously silent.

I was taking those last strides towards that French window when suddenly a premonition swept over me. I knew there'd be something wrong about that villa when we entered.

4

Joanou

I was right. We all crowded into the main room of that tiny mountain villa. Someone slammed the French window and shut out the storm.

But already I was plunging across to that inner room. The room with the clothes chest and divan bed.

For lovely, goddess-like Charmain wasn't in this room . . . and she wasn't in that bedroom either when I flung open the door. There was her wrap on the floor. But no Charmain.

I whirled in the doorway and looked at those wretched travellers from the bus. I was thinking: God, she must have been terrified to have gone out into this storm!

My eyes swept over those people standing there. I saw the peasant-type Cypriots. They'd be Turks, of course, wearing those black baggy pants and high leather boots. They had thin faces and long black moustaches. The men, anyway. The women were smaller counterparts of their dark-skinned, thin-faced menfolk. I began to realise there were six of them in this little party, all sodden wet and angry now in reaction to their recent discomfort. They were beginning to argue amongst themselves.

But my eyes went quickly to the others who had been travelling on that bus. There were things I wanted to know, wanted to find out. My ear was hurting me.

I looked at that big, blue-jowled prosperous Greek Cypriot. He was getting out of his suit coat, doing it distastefully, like a man who shuns the physical discomfort of wet sleeves. He looked frightened. I thought, thinking of B.G., big fellows were often like that. They hadn't the guts of normal-sized people.

The soft young Cypriot woman, another Greek Cypriot if I wasn't mistaken, was indulging in hysterics.

Her way of saying thanks for getting

out of that uncomfortable storm. Her clothes were clinging to her, shaping her form. They were less flattering when they were wet than when in drier moments. They showed the fullness of her breasts, and they were too full to be fashionable. And it gave her a big round stomach between massive thighs. Her elderly consort was hovering round her, trying to quiet her. He was getting excited, his brown eyes rolling dramatically, and he wasn't helping at all.

I looked at the two English spinster women. They were of sterner breed. They looked more delicate than all the others, and yet they were taking this situation docilely, almost impassively.

They were washed out, pathetic creatures. Their hair was down in stringy wetness about their thin unlovely faces. Their clothes, too, clung to their figures and there was not the young ripeness about them that gave the Greek-Cypriot girl at least some pretensions to comeliness. They made me think of penguins waddling about in their unfashionably long dresses that were made still longer by the weight of water in them.

And yet they began quietly pushing back their hair and making tiny adjustments to their appearance in those first few seconds while they relaxed gratefully in the warmth and comfort of that crowded lounge of the mountain villa.

The Armenian was recovering his breath. He was redder-faced, more apple-like than ever. Young. With plenty of go in him when he wanted.

Now he wanted. He said firmly: 'I'd better take charge.' He was a confident, cocky little so-and-so.

I found myself grinning a bit when I saw him come bouncing forward and looking fatly important. But he took himself seriously.

'We'll stay here for the night. Tomorrow someone will go down to Kyrenia and summon a relief coach.'

He looked round. Very firmly he looked at that big, uneasy-looking Greek Cypriot with the prosperous air and blue chin. He said: 'You can do it. Walking will do you a lot of good.' He was a right cocky little devil.

Then that Greek Cypriot turned and shouted in Greek at the Armenian. I didn't know what he said. Probably told him what he thought of the idea. And miraculously the confidence oozed out of that Armenian. He began to run away at once. He was gesturing with his hands, and his face was twisting into the semblance of a placating smile. He was saying things in Greek, and I didn't need to know the language to understand what he was saying.

It probably was: 'Okay, keep your hair on. I was only kidding. All right, if that's how you feel I'll go myself!'

I never saw a man come off his pedestal so quickly. That little Armenian, for all his bounce, hadn't the guts of a louse.

I came to an abrupt halt in my thoughts. I was saying to myself: 'Someone's missing.'

For a second I couldn't put a name to it, but subconsciously I was realising that a face wasn't there among that party. I cast my mind back, frantically trying to think. Then it came to me.

That thin-faced man with glasses and

the curiously white chin. He wasn't here with those passengers.

I found myself shouting almost: 'Someone's missing! That fellow with the glasses! A Britisher, I reckon. Where did he go?'

Though in my mind was the thought: How did he go?

For that night one man had already gone over the edge of the precipice. I was thinking: In the dark maybe something like that happened to him, too.

Everyone looked at each other and then looked back at me. There was consternation on their faces, the relief of a moment before wiped away by the horrifying implications of what we had just discovered.

Because we couldn't believe that a man would voluntarily stay out in that storm when there was this dry villa offering comfort and security.

The soft, rounded, Greek-Cypriot woman indulged in more hysterics. Someone translated and then the Turkish-Cypriots began to yammer excitedly together, the whites of their eyes rolling dramatically, and their hands talking right up to their elbows. A couple of their women began to cry in a high keening note, like people bewailing the dead.

The English women again showed sterner stuff. They didn't indulge in any dramatics. One of them stepped forward and said: 'Perhaps he couldn't keep up with us. He looked thin. He might have fallen and we never noticed it.' She looked around firmly, pushing back strands of wet hair with a thin, veined hand that trembled with cold. 'Someone must go out and look for him.'

No one moved. She marched resolutely towards the French window. 'I will go. Perhaps I'd better take that torch with me.'

Her companion began to go uncertainly after her. I heard her whisper softly: 'Oh, Frances, you'll never stand up to this storm again.'

I went after the game old bird and took her by her thin bony shoulders and brought her away from the French window. 'I'll go out in a few minutes,' I said. 'But you're not going out.' She wasn't fit for any more exhausting adventures, I could see. I wasn't, either, and I cursed at being committed to such an ordeal.

Then all the stranded passengers looked at each other. I looked at Keremetlian, that round little private eye who had elected himself leader of our party. I said, ironically: 'What now, chief?'

He just shrugged. His eyes flickered towards that blue-jowled Greek-Cypriot who had jumped on him. I knew what he was thinking. He wasn't going to stick his neck out again.

So I said: 'All right. The gals can go into the bedroom and dry themselves and get into any clothes and blankets they can find. The men can stay here and do the same. I'll get any men's clothing out of the closet first, however.'

I was in a hurry. There was that missing Greek girl, Charmain, on my mind. And I had to go out and look for the missing man with glasses. I didn't want to do it, but I'd promised and the sooner I got it over, the sooner I could climb out of these wet, clinging pants.

I went to the door of the bedroom. B.G. came and stood in the doorway looking after me. He wouldn't let me out of his sight now, I realised. He must have felt something comforting in the Heggy presence. I thought: The heck, I'm going to make something out of this or my name's not Heggy.'

The big slob had fired me for calling him names. And my job paid plenty dollars.

I opened one clothes closet. I was just thinking: In films when you open a cupboard door a body falls out.

The old Cat and the Canary stunt. There was a body inside that closet. A nice body.

Only there was warmth in it and it didn't fall dead on me.

It was Charmain.

I said: 'That's where you got to, is it? I might have known.' I didn't tell her the sarcasm that was in my mind — that I might have known she wouldn't have separated herself from those lovely clothes inside the closet.

She was looking at me with fear in her

eyes. I said: 'Nobody's going to hurt you, honey. Step right out. You can't stay in that clothes box all night.'

I handed her out of the closet in gallant style. I turned. B.G's fat mouth was open in wonder. He hadn't expected to see such a piece of bedding come out from among those hanging clothes. He took off his glasses and polished them as if to make sure he wasn't seeing things.

Charmain had changed in my absence. She was wearing slacks, well-shaped, expensive-looking dove-grey ones that suited her. She had on a simple cream blouse and a tiny bolero jacket of rich mulberry colour. And her hair was done up. She'd got into high heels again, too, and that suggestion of dumpiness that goes with all women in their bare feet had disappeared. Again she was tall and slim and elegant — and so inviting!

She wouldn't move from that closet door. Or couldn't move. Honestly, that girl was dead scared of what lay in the other room.

I couldn't waste a lot of time on her. We were all too uncomfortable to concern ourselves with somebody's imaginary fears. Or if they weren't imaginary, we still couldn't become too concerned about them.

I swept up all the men's clothes I could see hanging in that closet. Then I started to walk to where B.G. stood in the doorway. He moved aside. I felt that girl's hand grip on to the oilskin sleeve of my arm. It was painful, almost. She came through that doorway with me in the manner of a woman who wasn't going to be left alone.

I was thinking, ironically: I've got B.G. hanging on to me like a kid to his daddy. And now this dame does the same. Maybe Heggy's got something.

I decided in both cases if I could I would cash in on it. B.G. for my job back. The girl . . .

We went into that crowded room of damp, dejected people. All the time Charmain was clinging to me.

I got impatient, because she was still trying to hold me back. But as I turned and looked at her I saw her eyes sweeping that room, looking in fear at those people. And she was trembling.

I saw all that, and then, all in an

instant, she wasn't trembling any more. She wasn't afraid. Instead her hold relaxed on my sleeve, and when her eyes turned towards me they seemed to be ablaze with . . . triumph?

She smiled. Ever had a goddess smile at you? When she smiled she was ravishing. Big eyes, fine forehead, rather high cheekbones and small pointed chin. Ripe red lips and gleaming white teeth and that great crescent halo of gleaming black hair. She was a wow!

If I hadn't known she was a gal who'd been around I guess I might have tumbled for that smile.

I turned away from her. I was wondering: Now, why is she feeling good, suddenly?

It made her moments in that clothes closet a waste of time if after all she had nothing to fear from those bus passengers.

My eyes travelled over those people. I thought: I don't see much to fear among them. They were too wet and cold and miserable.

The Armenian jumped forward when he saw that bundle of clothes in my hands. 'Friend, I'll take charge of the distribution,' he said firmly. He was always ready to take charge of something, I was beginning to notice. I found it comical, but to date no one else had. Maybe these Cyprus people didn't go for that sort of thing like we Americans.

I gave him the clothes, all but for a good pair of pants. Then I jerked my head towards the bedroom.

'You ladies get in there and do for yourselves,' I told them, and there was a little more interpreting and then the women came drooping unhappily forward.

The big soft Greek Cypriot girl had to be helped by that fussy old man right up to the doorway. He might even have gone through with her but I kept him out.

I said: 'Leave little Mary to do her own chores. You grab yourself some pants and get into 'em.'

Goddamnit, right then B.G. set up a gripe. There were no curtains to the windows. People outside could see them changing, he argued, his eyes behind his prissy glasses very bright and his fat chin wobbling pathetically.

I said, sourly: 'There's no one outside interested in you, B.G. Outside there's only one person — the killer!'

Maybe the way I said it was offensive. Or maybe it was that word 'killer' that I'd used. I saw B.G. flinch and go away blinking. Though he didn't go very far away from me.

Then there was one helluva shindig, over where the Armenian was distributing the clothes. His authority once again was being questioned.

The customers hadn't been satisfied with the distribution and now, to his indignation, they were helping themselves. Those Turkish Cypriots in their black wet bloomers were taking what they fancied — and that Armenian had been sitting on the best clothes for himself.

I saw a flare up of temper immediately. Those lean brown long-moustached faces opened and shouted at the round little Armenian. He quailed before the fury of their angry, shouting voices, and he went back, but he tried to take his clothes with him.

The boys just up and got them and tore them from his grasp and he sat down and looked dejected, like a man who is frequently defeated and yet never gets used to the idea.

He came over to me and he was almost weeping. These Continentals are a demonstrative folk. 'Look, I am the distributor,' he wailed. 'And look what I get out of it.' He held up one pair of inelegant pants. He'd come out worst in the deal. He always came out worst in the deal, I thought, and I felt a warmth of sympathy for the little guy.

And then I thought: Maybe you upped and hit me on my ear! A curious thing to think, because the Armenian had been huddled back with all the other people at the bus when I went along with the lamp. I didn't see how he could have massaged my ear for me.

But someone had. And somehow I couldn't feel it was the killer who had done it.

That reminded me. I'd made a promise. I ducked out, looking for that Britisher. I was back in a few minutes. It was hopeless, trying to find anyone out in the blackness of that storm. I came back and said so.

We got dried, and changed. And then the inner door opened and the women came out. They looked ashamed of themselves and rather foolish, because they weren't all the same size and shape as the Greek girl whose clothes they were borrowing. The two English women had picked up blankets in addition, and wore them like Indian squaws around their shoulders. They were the quietest, most composed of them all. The soft young Greek-Cypriot woman saw that ageing man and promptly held out her arms and burst into tears like a child who wanted consoling.

She looked better now, in clothes that nearly fitted her, and I thought, maybe I wouldn't mind trying to console her myself.

With that thought I lifted my eyes and found myself staring into those rich brown ones of that Greek goddess, Charmain. I lay a dime to a grand she knew what was in my mind, too, because her lips compressed and she looked angry for a second.

Some food was rustled up. Charmain didn't help to get it. She told them where to find the food and coffee, and it was the two English spinsters who served it up for us. They appeared to be glad to do this little task and they did it well and quickly.

They were spinsters. That had emerged by now. Two misses. I couldn't tell which was which, but one was a Miss George, and the other a Miss Paterson.

In time, however, they did emerge as personalities. The smaller, frailer one with the subdued air was Miss Paterson. The other, with a more vigorous, decisive manner, was Miss George. Miss George had quite an amount of protective instinct in her, I could see, because she mothered her companion, watching all the time so that she could help her. More and more I began to respect those two British women.

I'd seen many like them around this part of the world. Women with microscopic incomes who settle far from the land they love in order to live in some sort of comfort. Usually they do a lot of good missionary work among the people where they live . . .

After we'd eaten, I began to feel the strain grow again upon our company. After a while I began to realise why, too. Then the soft young woman had hysterics and clung once more to her elderly consort. He wasn't her grandfather, we'd discovered. He was her husband. Good luck to her — and him, I thought, when I learned that. For it was a waste of good woman on ageing manhood.

Those hysterics affected all of us differently. The big Greek-Cypriot with the blue jowl, who was trying to dry the contents of his pocket over a kerosene stove that we'd lighted, jumped to his feet and he seemed to be on the edge of panic himself. His brown eyes rolled like Harpo Marx's and he dithered about a lot before settling back to his task again.

Some of the Turks began to moan and look fearfully over their shoulders.

Then we all settled down to look at that uncurtained window. We were all thinking that we couldn't see out into the storm that lashed those windows, but if the murderer — the killer of Christopholou and our unfortunate driver — was out there he would be able to watch our every movement.

Brother, it wasn't a nice feeling. I'm thick-skinned, insensitive usually, but I got the prickles down my spine at that thought.

And yet there was nothing we could do about it.

All the time Charmain kept close to me. In time I began to realise that she kept behind me. She saw to it that Joe P. Heggy was between her and those uncurtained windows that seemed about to crash in every time the shrieking storm-blast assaulted this lonely mountain villa.

I'd squatted in a corner because there weren't chairs enough to go round. Charmain, elegant in her slacks and bolero jacket, had come and sat against my shoulder. It was an invitation, I knew, and I put my arm round her. She didn't object. I figured, apart from everything else, she felt comforted to have a man's arm around her just then.

For Charmain still had that fear lurking behind her. She was a woman expecting something to happen — something horrible and brutal and perhaps encompassing herself.

I tried to get the truth out of her. Why she was afraid. She just sat and brooded like a lovely statue and never seemed to hear my questions. In time I realised that she was concentrating on listening — listening for sounds outside.

The other people, in spite of their fears, began to doze. I looked at my strap watch and was surprised to find it wasn't yet midnight. We seemed to have been in that storm for days, and not just an hour or so.

The big Greek-Cypriot, drying the contents of his wallet by the stove, must have been tired, too. His fingers grew clumsy, and part of the contents of that now dried wallet were dislodged and came fluttering towards where I sat against the wall. One was a card — a visiting card.

I was obliging. I picked it up to hand to the man, and then I caught a glimpse of the script name centred on that ivory panel.

It said Joanou.

5

The point of death

I handed that card back to the big, uneasy
Greek-Cypriot without saying a word.
But I was no longer sleepy. I was alert
and my mind was racing, trying to think
things out.

Joanou is as common a name in
Cyprus as Smith in Boston. But it was a
coincidence that that name should be
linked with this house owned by Christopholou, deceased.

I thought: I'm going to watch that guy.
Maybe he's got a good reason for being
uneasy.

I looked at his pocket. He was so heavy
with fat that he bulged everywhere, so
that staring at his pockets didn't tell me
anything. But I wondered if he had a gun
in one of them, transferred from his wet
clothes.

I got cramp in my muscles then, and

decided to walk into the kitchen to make coffee. I didn't intend to fall asleep that night, anyway. Charmain followed me. B.G. looked up as if he'd like to come with me, too, but he was too tired to lift himself from the ground and he stayed where he was. For once.

We went into the kitchen together. It was a small place. With a kerosene cooker. And water in a small tank.

Charmain drooped against the wall while I made coffee. She let me. She was the kind of flower who did no work at all if she could get away with it.

I made that coffee, and all the time I was thinking. I realised in time that she was thinking, too.

She came close up to me where I stood savouring the smell of fresh-ground coffee, and she put her hand into the small of my back and she was caressing me. She had a smart technique.

I waited for it.

She said, in a very small voice: 'I want to go to America.'

I measured out the coffee. 'Why?'

A shrug of those shapely shoulders

under that bolero. 'Nothing ever happens on this island.'

I cocked one eye at her. Two corpses in one night — maybe three — and she said nothing ever happened. She sure was hard to please.

She went on with this new idea of hers. 'I've got money.' She looked at me triumphantly, like someone pulling a big surprise.

I let the coffee boil. I said encouragingly: 'A lot?'

She nodded with quick enthusiasm. She thought the sucker was going for the bait.

'Thousands. And pounds, too, not dollars. I've been careful with the money I've received. I've put it all away.'

She spoke with fierce intentness. I guessed that she'd be careful with money — other people's . . .

I whistled. 'Thousands? That's money when you talk in pounds.' I stirred the coffee, letting it simmer. 'What about America?'

She did that face-averting act again. I'd got wise to it now. When she didn't want me to see her eyes she kept them aloof from me. Eyes sometimes tell stories.

She said: 'You're not married?' I suppose she could tell by my manner. I nodded. She seemed to sigh. 'If you marry me I become an American citizen?' Her voice was questioning, and now her eyes came up to read the answer on my face.

I nodded. 'Yep. I reckon marrying me would make you a United States' citizen. And you're not the only one who wants to stand under the Stars and Stripes.' I paused, thinking.

She was getting warm now. That hand behind my back had stolen to the back of my neck and was fondling it as if she loved it. Maybe she did at that moment. And I liked it, and if it did her any good she could go on playing with my golden locks.

'Will you marry me?'

I considered the matter, stirring the coffee. She went on quickly, trying to sell me: 'All that money — think what we could do with it in America!'

I thought about it.

She said: 'Well?'

So I told her the truth. 'Honey, you're all right for a time. A nice time. But marrying you — ' I shook my head.

The hand had been swiftly withdrawn from my neck. Those warm, eager eyes had gone rigid and cold, staring at me.

I stared back. I said: 'Sister, you're poison ivy. I figure men don't stay alive long when once they've had your arms around them.' She went conventional. She drew back her hand to slap my face. Oh yeah, they get the Hollywood movies in Cyprus, too.

But I didn't stand there to have my face slapped, not even by someone as lovely as Charmain. I ducked and let it ride over me, and in the same movement I shoved her on one side and put out the lamp above the stove. I did it very quickly. That last sentence of mine had put an idea into my mind.

She got the wrong idea. I heard her go quickly back in the darkness, and I heard a sharp exclamation, 'Oh!'

I don't know what she expected. I suppose some sort of amorous approach.

She figured there could be only one reason for putting out a lamp, and after what I'd said she wasn't going to play.

She got me wrong . . . for once.

I went jumping towards the small window that gave out onto the storm beyond the kitchen.

I'd seen someone standing out there, but I knew I wouldn't see him or her so well while that lamp was alight, because you can't see into darkness with a light shining behind you. So putting the lamp out made the night outside, if anything, lighter than the kitchen, and I could see.

Quickness paid off. I saw.

For a fraction of a second I saw a shadowy, brooding figure out there in the storm. A formless shape that could have been someone with a coat over his . . . or her . . . head. A shape that had been standing a yard back from the window, watching me with Charmain.

I saw that figure in a flash of lightning, and then the blue light snapped off and there was darkness beyond as profound as here in the kitchen.

The next flash of lightning revealed

. . . nothing. The bird had ducked out.

The coffee boiled over. Charmain flung open the door to the lounge and yellow light streamed in. She stood in the rectangle of light, looking at me, and it threw shadows on her face and made it look interesting. She was staring at me, wondering. Not understanding.

I lit the lamp and mopped up the coffee. Then I put it in the coffee pot and poured it out. A cup for me. A cup for Charmain.

While I poured in sugar and stirred it I said: 'The finger's on me now, sweet-heart.'

She didn't understand. So I explained. 'You remember what I was saying to you? That you've got the kiss of death, honey?' She had shut the door now, and was standing in the middle of the kitchen watching me. There was no smile on those flawless features. No warmth. Nothing to make a man want her, for all her beauty. Just a primitive, scheming woman listening so that she could turn what she heard to her advantage.

I sighed. The coffee was good. It had

the Heggy touch, I told myself. Aloud I said: 'The last thing I said before you took a poke at me was that when you put your arms around a man it's time to send him a wreath.'

I jogged her memory. Yangos Joanou, deceased. He was boyfriend Number One, that I knew of. And then Christopholou — the late lamented Boyfriend Number Two. 'Now,' I told her evenly, 'Boyfriend Number Three seems likely to have the name of Joe P. Heggy and, sweetheart, I sure don't like it.'

She stood there, not touching the coffee I'd given her.

She was trying to assimilate what I was saying. So I explained even further, more patiently.

I waved my steaming coffee cup towards the kitchen window. 'There was a guy out there. He was out in the storm, watching us in this kitchen. He saw me standing here, letting you stroke my curly hair.' That was swank. The Heggy hair doesn't curl. 'Figure out what that means, honey, if the spectator was the gent I reckon he is.'

Her hand went to that lipsticked mouth of hers. It opened and I saw the whiteness of her teeth within. I'll swear her face blanched, and her frightened brown eyes swung swiftly towards that window. She took a step towards me. Whenever she was scared, no matter how much she hated my guts, she came close to me to find protection.

She whispered: 'There was someone out there?'

I nodded. 'A man — I think.'

She whispered: 'A man. You think. The killer of Chris and the bus driver.' She shuddered. She was in a panic, suddenly weak about the knees, I reckon. She said, desperately: 'You're right in what you say. If I was seen . . . just then . . . stroking your head, you'll be the next to die.'

I got my mouth out of that hot coffee, choking and spluttering. I griped: 'The heck, next time you say a thing like that just see that a man isn't drinking hot coffee. It's enough to make a fellow choke!' I was indignant.

But I was also watching that window and thinking how easy it was to shoot down someone through glass.

With that thought I moved into the lounge. Charmain followed me. B.G. felt flattered. I went and sat closer to him than I'd ever done in his life before. He was big and fat, and there wasn't an inch of me showing from those windows that faced south onto the Kyrenia road.

Charmain sat beside me. She was going to be my shadow while ever this night lasted. I didn't blame her.

But I turned and I said to her: 'It's time you opened up, baby. You know a lot. Give. Who killed Christopholou?'

She looked at me in surprise then. As if I ought to have guessed. Then she shrugged. She told me: 'Haverford — the editor who was sent to jail.' Then she added viciously, nastily: 'The fool!'

My mind flew to that arty, bearded gent featured in the Cyprus paper. I thought: That's logical. He'd be out now. He must have been waiting on that trail, and he got Christopholou when the headlights fell on him.'

But I couldn't understand why Haverford had thrown the Cypriot to his death.

What was there about the bus driver for the killer to fear?

I suddenly remembered what the driver had said. Something about his driving mirror. But I didn't get anywhere with that thought.

I began to get the idea that the storm was abating. No longer did it seem as though the roof was going to take off or the windows to burst in on us under the impetus of a rain-laden wind. There seemed to be pauses now between the fury of those blasts.

I began to think it would be quickly over. Storms are like that in Cyprus. I've got a feeling the people are a bit like it, too.

Charmain was nestling up against me. I knew she hadn't given up the attack. She'd been affronted, but she wasn't going to let that stand in the way of her ambitions.

She turned on the charm. She kept close to me, so that I could feel the warmth of her lovely, soft young body as it pressed against mine. I got that perfume in my nostrils again.

100

It did things to me. I got my arm back around her. I wasn't going to let a little quarrel stand in the way of pleasure. She wasn't, either. It was quite a tender moment, sitting close against the lovely Greek girl, my arm round her slim waist — and both keeping up close to the protective bulk of the snoozing B.G.

Most other people were snoozing now. I looked round. It was as if with the lessening of the fury of that storm they began to feel they were out of the wood.

The apple-like Armenian was curled up in a chair. He'd got himself the best one in the room. The other chairs were all occupied by women. The Turkish Cypriots were nodding, leaning against each other on their chairs for support. Their menfolk were sprawling, down on the floor. They looked the hardy kind, able to sleep anywhere. They were sleeping now, heedless of any possible menace in the storm outside. And they were snoring.

The big, blue-jowled Greek Cypriot with the name of Joanou was huddled uncomfortably in a corner. He wasn't sleeping much, and kept coming awake and sitting up and staring at that rain-washed French window. I could sense the fear in the man, and I felt there was a greater depth to it than I'd first imagined. I wanted to know who this Joanou was . . .

The two English women were sitting uncomfortably upright on their chairs. Quaint figures with those blankets draped round their narrow, bony shoulders.

The woman called Frances — that would be Miss George — was very solicitous, guarding her companion. She was holding her thin, veined, worn hands and whispering to her. I had a feeling she was the stronger of the two and was mothering her companion. I felt there was more to this Miss George than I'd first imagined.

She was tougher than most of us, I was realising. But her strength came from this protective instinct in her, which manifested itself in attending to her companion's comfort and disregarding her own.

The soft-looking Greek woman with the elderly husband was being petulant.

She couldn't get comfortable in her chair and she made baby noises of protest. Her elderly husband was continually having to get up and make her more comfortable in a chair that was next only to the Armenian's in luxury. With all that fat on her she should have been able to sleep anywhere.

The old man, all the same, was pretty ardent. I thought cynically that to get a ripe young woman at his age must have done his glands a lot of good. I could see the way he touched her and stroked her he could hardly keep his hands off the prize he had got. The thought suddenly occurred to me they might just have been married. This might even have been the start of his honeymoon.

I grinned. He must have been hating us all like hell, if that was so. I reckon I would have been, in his place.

I got tired of looking around and thinking. There was such a lot I wanted to know. Charmain had said that the editor — former editor now, doubtless — of a British newspaper in Cyprus was responsible for the Christopholou killing. Which made him probably responsible for the murder of our Cypriot bus driver.

I thought of that other missing man, the man with glasses and the small, pointed chin. I wondered what had happened to him. Maybe he'd run into the crazy Editor Haverford and gone the way of the Cypriot, I thought.

I said softly to Charmain; 'You say he was a fool.' She knew who I was referring to. Her brow contracted and her lips set, and her face looked stony and yet angrily so.

I whispered: 'What was wrong with him?'

Her eyes flickered round to mine. She had good eyes. She said, almost sulkily; 'He was British and a writer. Isn't that enough?'

I thought of that arty beard in that picture and I began to nod. Maybe I did understand.

'He thought himself a little tin god?'

'More than that.' Her voice was again vicious. 'He thought being editor put him above all other people. He thought it gave him rights. He was a man infatuated by a little power.'

I nodded. My voice was approving. 'You sure are a character reader. What did he do? Pick on you?'

She nodded sombrely. 'He saw me and wanted me.' Her lips made an unpleasant moue. As if the thought filled her with distaste.

'You didn't . . . lead him on . . . just a bit?'

She said: 'No!' snappily. But she pulled her eyes away from mine, quickly, and I knew she wasn't on the level. I guess Charmain couldn't resist the advances of a man at any time. Not even when she was living with another man. In this case the ill-fated Yangos Joanou.

She said: 'It made him unpleasant because I wouldn't have anything to do with him. In the end he was made to realise it.'

I fenced. I felt that I was beginning to get towards the truth now. I could see it even through Charmain's half-truths. I made her go on talking about the incident.

'Haverford came up to my apartment in Nicosia late one night. He had been drinking. He wouldn't understand when I told him I couldn't have anything to do with him.' Her eyes flickered across to me. 'I was expecting Yangos to return any time. He had gone to one of his . . . meetings.'

I lay back against that wall, feeling for a cigarette. I was picturing that scene. Charmain trying to get rid of a conceited, egotistical British newspaper editor. Maybe she'd led him on and he'd come on a lot faster than she'd reckoned on. He was there and trying to cash in on promise, and she must have been frantic, expecting her lover to return any time.

'He got hold of me.' Charmain shuddered. And yet I was sure many a man had had hold of her. 'He wouldn't let me go. The more I struggled the more unpleasant he got.'

I thought: But you could have shouted for help.

Then I thought there might have been reasons for not doing so. I could think of a lot, right then, some of them bound up with Joanou's political associations.

Crudely I asked: 'Well, go on, what happened?'

Her head came round with eyes that bit into me with anger at that. She didn't draw away. 'Joanou came in time.'

'And Joanou?' I knew these Cypriot lovers. They become very dramatic.

There was satisfaction in Charmain's voice. 'Yangos thrashed Haverford. He thrashed him so hard Haverford couldn't ever forget it. The worst of it was he was thrashed while I was made to look on. Haverford's pride couldn't stand that.'

She was telling the truth then. I could see that. And I could imagine the fury of a man like Haverford humbled before the woman he desired. It was something that would promote undying hatred.

Well, it had done. Haverford had somehow got to know that Joanou, along with Christopholou, had been behind the attempted assassination — an assassination in which a poor devil of a local government servant had lost his life . . .

I suddenly sat so stiffly erect that Charmain was shunted onto her back on the floor. I was remembering something, something I had missed. My eyes went across that room, looking for someone. It was the smaller, the frailer, more pathetic of the two Englishwomen.

My eyes dropped to the handbag each held on her knees before her. They were big handbags. They could carry quite bulky articles.

Charmain said anxiously: 'What is it? What startled you?'

I looked at her. Then I said: 'I don't think there's anyone else in this room who knows your name is Charmain or knows who you are — Yangos Joanou's former mistress.'

She let the mistress word ride, though many a woman wouldn't have done. She knew I was deadly serious about something. She said: 'Why do you say that?'

I shrugged: 'Just keep it to yourself, honey. I figure you might find things a whole lot more uncomfortable if somebody here gets to know your identity.' My eyes went across to those two Englishwomen again.

Deliberately I brought the subject back to this killer of Christopholou and the Cypriot.

'Christopholou was killed because

Editor Haverford knew you were living with him and he couldn't stand the thought.'

She nodded, and again her eyes grew sombre. 'Men are like that,' she said viciously. 'Some men. When they go crazy over a woman they eat their hearts out if they think she is being shared by some other man.'

I said, comfortably: 'Don't include me among those saps, baby. I like women. But I don't make a fool of myself over them. I reckon there's not much difference between most women, and I don't put any on a pedestal. If I can't get a woman I want I don't try. You can remember that.'

Charmain shrugged cynically. Her lovely dark hair came sweeping over her rounded cheekbones at that, brushing my face and leaving that curious feeling that always remains when a woman's hair has touched a man. She wasn't going to take offence at anything I said now.

I guess she still had it in her mind that she'd make me somehow, and in the end she'd become a United States' citizen. So that she could go to God's Own Country as Mrs. Heggy.

She had a hope.

I thought I'd shake her out of her complacency. I said: 'Do you know that guy's name?' I nodded towards the uneasily sleeping Joanou.

I saw Charmain's brow furrow as she looked at him. As if there was something about him she should recognise. But she shook her head and again her hair caressed my face. That hair was doing more for Charmain than all her persuasive talk. It was getting to make me want to . . . please her.

I said, drily: 'The name's Joanou.'

I saw her eyes open. Suddenly there was uncertainty in them, as if my words smashed a firmly held theory. I heard her say, quickly: 'Then it could have been him. He might have killed Chris . . . '

I was startled. Then I recovered. I told her: 'You forget one thing. He was on the bus when Chris was killed.'

Her lovely face came round to look at me, and once again there was pitying contempt in her big brown eyes. It riled me. I could see she knew things that I still didn't know, and I wanted to know them. I didn't like the thought of being less smart than a girl.

I began to say: 'What's burning you, sister?'

But she was full of questions herself. She was looking at that big Cypriot with the rounded chin that needed a shave. Her eyes were alert and, I thought, apprehensive. 'You sure you haven't made a mistake? Do you know . . . his first name?'

'Hagop. That's his name. Does that . . . confirm anything?'

She nodded slowly. It seemed that knowing the worst somehow reassured her. A contradiction in terms and yet possible. She whispered: 'Yes. There is a resemblance.' She looked at me quickly. 'That's Yangos Joanou's brother.'

I shrugged. 'That was my guess. So what?'

Her eyes went to the polished wood floor. I was beginning to think it was the hardest floor I'd ever rested on.

I heard her words and they came softly

to my ear only. 'He didn't like it
. . . about Chris, I mean. When Yangos
was imprisoned Chris took me in.' Her
eyes fluttered, lifted to meet mine, but
didn't quite reach my level. In other
words, she avoided my glance.

'They hadn't liked Yangos having a — '

' — a mistress?' I helped her out.

She avoided confirming the phrase.
Women are always like that. She went on:
'But when I went to Chris I heard that
the Joanou family were angry about me
and said hard things.' Her eyes did meet
mine now, but for only a second. She
pouted. 'But Chris was so kind. And he
was lonely, hiding out from the police. I
felt I wasn't harming Yangos to go and
live with him.'

I shrugged: 'Maybe you were right at
that. I wouldn't know. You just don't pick
your boyfriends very carefully, that's my
only comment.'

I looked across at Joanou. I suppose it
wasn't remarkable that Hagop Joanou
had never met his brother's mistress. Men
like to keep their mistresses away from
their families. I thought: Here's another

who's going to react if he gets to know Charmain's identity.

There were at least two people in that room who might be unpleasant with the girl because of her past associations. She was in a tight spot.

I told her so, again. 'You're on the spot, baby. Just keep your name out of things. Maybe when the sun shines tomorrow everyone will go away and you'll have come to no harm.'

Then I thought of that killer somewhere out in the dying storm on that mountainside. I thought: He won't leave her alone. A man like Editor Haverford, full of pride and wounded vanity, could be mighty awkward. I guessed he'd stay around until he'd acquitted himself in the eyes of his beloved. Those guys always do.

I thought he'd committed himself too far already. I mean, killing two people in one night. My thoughts went back to that Cypriot bus driver. I could understand Christopholou being killed — he was enjoying the favours of the woman Editor Haverford wanted. But that cheerful, skilful bus driver — what did he know that had made him suddenly a danger to the killer?

Charmain could have told me right then. I didn't know this until later. Maybe she didn't quite understand herself at the time. But she could have told me, only she didn't. It turned out to be mighty unpleasant for a few of us, that reticence.

A couple of hours passed. The people in that room were mostly asleep now, though it was an uneasy sleep, made fitful by the conditions imposed by that crowded room. True there was a divan bed in the next room, but no one wanted to use it. I suppose they were all scared to be in a room apart from the crowd.

Both Englishwomen were awake still. Miss George had her arm round her companion's shoulders, I knew who that companion was now.

I was dozing myself when I heard Charmain get to her feet. I lay against the wall, my head uncomfortably drooping on my chest. I heard the door close. I had an impression of other movement. Time passed.

B. G. got up. He stretched and felt better for it. Maybe he didn't feel too bad, but then he had plenty of fat and that made sitting on a hard floor less uncomfortable than for people of the Heggy build, which runs more to bone and muscle.

The sap insisted on being friendly. I didn't want it. I kept my eyes shut as he got down again by my side. But he wanted to talk.

He talked. I heard his whisper: 'I've been thinking, Joe.'

I got one eye open. 'If it's about my job — ?'

He waved a fat paw. I was more concerned than I let him see. He said, generously: 'You know I didn't mean it, Joe.' I shut my eye, relieved. I was back in work again.

'Only, Joe, don't call me names like that again.' The boss's voice was plaintive. 'You know I don't like it.' I grunted. Now that I was in work again, I thought irritably: Why the hell doesn't he let a guy sleep?

But B.G. had something on his mind. I

was wondering where Charmain had got to.

B.G. said: 'I'm not sure I did right, Joe, in leaving Turkey when I did. I mean, it looked bad, don't you think, running out the way I did?'

I got my most cynical eye open. I knew what he was thinking. More, I knew why he was thinking it, and there I was a jump ahead of B.G.

I grunted: 'That fee-male's on your mind?'

He seemed to wince. I watched that fat face with those impressive big shot's octagonal-edged glasses. He was almost simpering, and there's nothing more sickening than a simper on a fat, middle-aged man's face.

'You mean Miss Dunkley?'

'I mean Lav.' Miss Dunkley had another name. Lavinia Dunkley. To the boys — B.G.'s construction crew on a U.N.O. job in Turkey — she was just plain Lav.

She was pretty plain. Not so young, nothing to look at, and yet all there when you examined her critically. She was another English spinster type. She had come into money and she'd started to travel abroad, and now suddenly she was determined to make up for the lost years.

She was a frustrated, love starved female, and the Mediterranean moon did things to her. She'd got a yen for B.G., and she'd chased the poor devil all over Istanbul in an effort to get him. And she'd got him.

That was why we'd come to Cyprus. B.G. was terrified she might get him again.

To a man like myself, I didn't understand it at all. I knew I'd never run away from a woman under any circumstances. Or I thought so, sitting uncomfortably there in that villa, with my spine feeling bruised and aching. I was to change my mind later.

But B.G. isn't an ordinary man, and little Lav had picked a bad type for her gauche experiments in l'amour.

For B.G. was an introverted, inhibited mass of humanity — and quite a mass, too. He too wasn't young, but he was full of illusions. Always he used to bleat that he was saving himself up for when the right woman came along. The boys used to take his pants away for that. With all the women dancing around us, we couldn't see how B.G. was going to recognise the right woman if she did come along.

But B.G. was sure little Lav wasn't the right woman. I suppose the guy had some picture in his sentimental heart of an entirely different woman-type. He'd done his best to run away from this little English spinster, but one time he hadn't run. He couldn't run. The boys had tanked him full of alcohol and got him pried loose from his inhibitions.

In that expansive feeling that comes with drunkenness, B.G. had gone up to show the timid but persistent little Lavinia that he was a man.

She been delighted. She'd been working for this moment for a long time.

We reckoned he had shown her, too, because with morning's sober light B.G. had been a trembling, contrite wreck.

He reckoned he had done wrong. He didn't believe in affairs like this, and he groaned in spirit and called himself a sinner.

I tried to help him. I kept pointing out that Lavinia wasn't groaning, that she had the kind of smile on her face that comes to a cat with a surfeit of milk.

He'd had to get out of sight of her, and so he'd dragged me all the way across to Cyprus for an unnecessary vacation.

I dropped an eyelid on my cynicism. I didn't want to see that fat face looking into the distance with bright, shining eyes.

Charmain still wasn't back, but I guessed where she was.

B.G. dug me in the ribs. I didn't open any eyes this time. I didn't want to hear what I knew he'd say. But he said it, all the same.

There was a fond, musing note in his voice. 'I think I misjudged Miss Dunkley,' he said. 'I mean, she had a rare and beautiful philosophy.'

I got my eyes open then. I'd never heard it called that before.

B.G. didn't see me glowering at him. He went on: 'She understands me. I feel somehow fine when I am with her. I think I could return to her now and not have any of that carnal spirit that disturbed me before.'

I risked that job I'd just got back. I grunted: 'Quit kidding yourself. You know what you're really thinking?'

He flushed. I was dead right.

I said: 'You're thinking of that night when you went to her. The more you think of it the more you remember you liked it. Now you want to get back to her because you want another night like that.'

B.G. looked indignant. He looked at me as if I had a lousy mind. I hadn't. I don't kid myself.

'Joe, you don't know me to say things like that — '

'By heck, I know men.' I wriggled up against the wall. 'And I know women, too,' I said acidly. 'Little Lav — she's got no fine and beautiful spirit. She's a woman who has come to her senses pretty late in life. She knows now what she was made for, and she is realising what a lot of fun she's missed in her thirty-odd years.'

He was going red and twiddling his fat fingers and trying to interrupt. I wouldn't let him. Dammit, he'd started this conversation and I wasn't going to listen to his flannelling.

'If you're a man, B.G., you'd admit it, too. And you'd quit running away from that dame and you'd go back there and make her a happy woman.'

B.G. jerked his head away. 'Out of marriage? That would be sin.'

'Good old sin!' I eased my aching back again. 'Why not marry the gal?'

He still wouldn't look at me. 'I'm waiting for the right woman to come along, and I don't think it's Miss Dunkley.'

His voice was full of dignity. I descended to sarcasm. 'Yeah, I've heard all that before.' I flipped a paw. 'You're saving yourself up until the right woman comes along.' I fixed him again with the Heggy eye. 'I guess you cashed in your life's savings at Istanbul last week. Looks like you've got to start saving all over again.'

B.G. turned a crimson face towards

me. He almost yapped: 'You've got no delicacy, Heggy.'

I didn't want any. I was going to say so. And then, in the kitchen, Charmain began to scream — the scream of a woman who is at the point of death.

6

She's poison

I was running towards that kitchen door. While I was running I was remembering that someone else went into the kitchen after Charmain.

I'd vaguely noticed it while I'd tried to sleep. I hadn't time to turn and check up on the occupants of that lounge now.

The others were jumping to their feet, reacting typically. I heard someone start screaming, and I knew it would be that soft young Greek-Cypriot woman. She'd be clinging to that ancient husband of hers.

Everyone else was talking excitedly. The Armenian fell off his chair.

I burst open the kitchen door. Charmain was up against a wall, her arms flung wide, her terror-stricken eyes crossed as they looked down at a knifepoint held to her throat.

Holding that knife was Miss George.

Miss George was saying nothing, but her face was very white and her faded grey eyes were intense as she stared at that glamorous woman trying to press her way back through a solid wall.

I slammed the kitchen door behind me then. I thought I could handle this situation. I walked over to Miss George.

I said, easily: 'Now, you don't intend to use that knife, do you?'

Faded grey eyes looked at me, but the knife didn't move away from Charmain's lovely throat. Miss George spoke firmly. Spinster women from England are often very decisive when they speak.

She said: 'I'm not so sure. I think the world might be well rid of her.'

I took the knife away from her, and she didn't resist. Charmain relaxed, and I thought she was going to fall to the floor. I stuck an arm round her and held her up.

Miss George said: 'I wouldn't go near that woman if I were you. She's not good for men.'

I said: 'I've got ideas like that myself about her. You know who she is?'

She nodded.

'How?'

Miss George's hands were trembling now with reaction to the violence she had displayed only a few seconds before. She turned away. She was ashamed of herself. She said: 'I saw a picture in the lounge when we came in. I kept it from . . . Miss Paterson. There was a name on it.'

I nodded. Charmain's picture in this villa . . . Christopholou's corpse out on the roadway. And the name Charmain. All things added up even in a spinster's mind.

Miss George whirled and faced me and her eyes were filling with emotion again. Only, this time there was indignation in them. And anger.

'When I saw that name, Charmain, I knew who she was. I knew what she was. She is the cause of misery to people. Her lover shot — '

' — Miss Paterson's brother?' It was a guess I made. I knew I was right.

Miss George nodded. I shoved Charmain towards the kitchen door. She went gladly into the lounge where other people were. I wanted to speak a little longer with Miss George.

She was trembling violently now. I put my hands on her shoulders and in a few moments the action seemed to brace her. She looked at me gratefully.

'You're a cynical American,' she said. An uncertain smile came to her face. She was quite a nice-looking person when the strain was away from her drawn features. 'But like most cynical people, you are good-hearted and sentimental.'

She caught me by the arms. She meant well. She said, earnestly: 'Let an old woman warn you, Mr. American. Keep away from that woman. Some women just naturally bring trouble upon their menfolk. Charmain has done it all her life, from what I've heard — even before Yangos Joanou — and I suppose she will go on bringing trouble.'

I shook my head slowly. 'I told you before, you don't need to lose any sleep over me. You've seen me with my arm round her.' I nodded vigorously. 'Sure you saw me. I never tried to keep it hidden from you. But that doesn't make me a sucker, Miss George. I just like putting my arm around a girl's waist.'

Her eyes lit up and she smiled at my frank statement. She wasn't affronted by it, either — she understood.

'But I don't lose my head over a pretty face.'

Miss George turned away and became feminine and did things to her hair. She wanted to talk to me.

'It's nice to talk to someone like you — what's your name?'

'Heggy. Call me Joe, though.'

'You're a strong-minded person, Joe. I think Charmain will meet her match in you. It will probably be the first time. She's let her beauty lure men to their doom. That English editor — Haverford. She got him hopelessly infatuated when Yangos Joanou was her lover.'

I nodded. This wasn't Charmain's story, but I reckoned it was more accurate than the Greek girl's.

'And they say that Yangos Joanou wouldn't have been so rash if he hadn't been inflamed to madness by the girl. He wanted to show off. Young men so often do. And it's so easy for them to think it's heroic to pick up a gun and go out and shoot someone.'

I was watching her as she spoke. I felt she wasn't condemning the dead Yangos. She was pitying him. Pitying him because she knew what perils there were with impulsive youth. And Charmain could make men impulsive.

Those grey eyes became bitter. 'I blame that girl. 'She made men dance, by all accounts. She was like a petulant child. Men made fools of themselves trying to win her pleasure, but she was never satisfied. That's how she kept her men, I suppose. She made them do things for her and while men do things they are caught. It's when they get what they want without having to do anything for it they begin to lose interest.'

She was a spinster but she knew a lot, that English woman. I thought of the old man outside, going frantic to please that big, soft young woman. He'd be lucky when he passed out and escaped from her, I thought cynically.

I looked at Miss George and I said:

'You blame this girl for everything. I don't agree with you altogether — '

'But then you're a man and she's a lovely woman.'

I nodded. 'And your sympathies are all taken up with poor Miss Paterson who lost her brother?'

'He was a fine man.' The spinster's hand trembled again and her voice was fierce as she spoke. 'I've known them ever since they came to Cyprus. We were great friends. I feel the loss almost as much as Hilda. This tragedy has just about broken her. We are going for a holiday to Kyrenia in order to try to forget.'

'And if she knows the woman in the case is in this house, that she's been living here with Christopholou?' I was interested in the reactions of this woman to the affair. Interested especially to see how her hatred was poured upon the member of her own sex involved. I couldn't go all the way with Miss George's strictures, but I could understand them.

She didn't say anything. Her eye must have seen that kitchen knife, because at once she began to apologise. 'I made a fool of myself. I came in here after her, wanting to tell her what I thought of her and her kind. Then I seemed to lose my head and I really felt that I wanted to kill her — the wanton!'

I patted her on the shoulder. 'Forget about it. We all do crazy things at times. But you're not cut out for violence and it's hurt you more than it hurt Charmain.'

She nodded, and then went out of the kitchen, her head bowed. Everyone looked up as we came in. Charmain was standing against the wall by B.G., her face showing signs of apprehension. Miss Paterson was sitting bolt upright on her chair, her face bewildered. I don't think she understood what was happening at all. Miss George went across and sat by her side and took her hands.

I got down beside B.G. This was one helluva night. I was griping to myself.

Then Hagop Joanou must have got tired of matching a hard wooden flooring with his backside. He got up and he was in a temper. The little Armenian had closed his eyes and was curled comfortably in a big chair.

Suddenly he found himself yanked off it. Hagop Joanou wasn't going to let him have all the comforts all the night.

Keremetlian started to bellyache. He was truculent about losing his chair and he did a lot of shouting. Then Joanou came half out of the chair, his big fist raised as if to smack the little Armenian down. There was dirty passion in those angry brown eyes.

Keremetlian seemed to collapse. He backed away from the threat, and he said things in Greek that were doubtless designed to placate the bigger man. Then he came and sat next to me and seemed to be brooding over the indignity of his position.

I kept my eyes on Joanou. I was learning a lot just by watching. Keremetlian's fear. Joanou's dirty passion. An ugly man, Joanou. A coward, but a man capable of doing brutal things to weaker people, I summed him up.

Charmain couldn't sit beside me now that Keremetlian was there. She stood against the wall, watching. I looked at her once and I knew she was wanting to say something with her eyes. I didn't fall for it. I just wanted to rest until daylight. Joe P. Heggy was a very tired man.

The Armenian took off his shoes. It wasn't really necessary. You could see his feet through the bottoms, anyway. He didn't wear socks.

Then he began to gripe in my ear. 'I know that fellow. I knew them all.' He looked at me cunningly. 'You know who he is?' He nodded towards heavy, sullen-looking Joanou.

I said, tiredly: 'Yeah. I know.'

Keremetlian wanted to talk. I didn't. But I couldn't shut him up. He whispered in my ear: 'They're all as bad as each other. All that family of Joanou's. Don't forget, mister, I know what I'm talking about.' His pride began to swell back again. He wasn't down long, that Armenian. 'I'm a dick, don't forget,' he said bumptiously.

'Sure, you're a dick,' I repeated mechanically. A dick who couldn't keep a sole on his shoes, I thought.

And yet I rather liked this little, round-apple of an Armenian, who seemed not to have grown up mentally. Maybe it's nice to find naive, simple people like Girais Keremetlian occasionally. I meet too many of the other kind.

I looked up. I was thinking that Charmain was on the other side of the fence. She had moved across to the door of the empty bedroom. She gave an almost imperceptible jerk of her head towards that room. I pretended I didn't see it. I wasn't in the mood for anything except just letting time go painlessly by until we could get the hell out of this place and find a soft bed in Kyrenia. I was thinking, with a mental groan, that tomorrow was going to be a tough day. There'd be police around asking questions. And we'd have to keep in the area in case they wanted us. I sighed.

Then I heard Keremetlian whisper; 'I know something.' I opened one eye. I guessed it looked like a fish's. He wasn't disconcerted and that cunning look remained on his round, cheerful face. 'I know there was more than Christopholou and Yangos Joanou in that plot.'

I said: 'Hell, everyone knows it. There

was a political organisation behind it. Christopholou and Joanou were the volunteers for the dirty job. The big fellows patted 'em on the back and said they were heroes. One of the heroes was hanged and the other stopped a bullet tonight.'

The Armenian was pulling on my sleeve urgently and his eyes were looking across at Hagop Joanou. Joanou seemed to have sunk into his fat chin, resting on his chest. He seemed to be asleep.

The Armenian whispered: 'Yes, but who were the organisers, the people behind those two young hotheads?'

I jerked my eyes open. I was looking at Joanou. 'You mean — '

The Armenian looked pleased with himself. 'Hagop Joanou is one of the ringleaders. He stood to make a lot of money if the British were made to quit the island. He's a politician and he's onto several grafts that he could develop if there weren't Britishers on this island. And there are others. But Joanou is one of the big men.'

I turned to look at that Armenian. I

134

was incredulous. 'You know all this. But the police don't.'

'The police suspect. I know.' He was almost bursting with pride. I saw him wriggle his bare toes with satisfaction. They were very dirty toes.

I looked doubtfully at him. That always makes them talk. 'Come off it,' I said. 'You don't get me to believe that.'

He shrugged. He was sure of himself. 'I get around,' he said. 'I get to know things. Everyone on the island seems to know, except the police.'

I nodded a bit at that. I felt there was truth in what he said. In these small communities often a whisper reaches everybody's ears before the police's. Maybe Keremetlian knew something after all. But where did this get us?

Joanou looked unpleasant and bad-tempered, trying to find comfort for his big body in that chair. But he didn't look formidable — not the ringleader of a group of anarchists. I thought, though, he might be. He had that cowardly streak which often makes men resort to violence. Especially gets them to inspire violence in others.

I said: 'You want to go and tell the police what you know.'

Keremetlian looked mockingly at me. 'And get bumped off by the Joanou mob?'

I nodded. I began to understand now why everyone knew except the police. The Joanou mob wouldn't be kind to informers. I reckoned this Armenian was sticking his neck out more than considerable in opening his yap to me.

But then he was the kind. He hadn't altogether grown up. He just couldn't keep things to himself, I figured.

Then my head slewed round slowly to look at that barefooted little man. A stabbing suspicion had come into my brain. I was thinking maybe he wasn't as naive as he looked. Maybe he was trying to put thoughts into my mind, thoughts that suited him.

Charmain was getting impatient. She wanted me to go across to her. I got pins and needles and that made me rise, so I went across to where she was standing. She didn't speak, but turned at once and went into that bedroom. The lamp was still burning. She stood just within the door, hidden from view of anyone looking in at that window by the projecting clothes closet.

I let the door swing to behind me. I realised that that girl was on tension. She was facing me, her hands gripped into tight balls of fists. Her face was paler than I'd seen it before, and her eyes looked bigger and were shining with a curious intensity. It wasn't fear that was in them, but it was some emotion close to it.

I complained: 'You pick a bad time to get a fellow into your bedroom.'

She said in a whisper: 'Don't be a fool. I've just been thinking.'

I said: 'Yeah?' But my question was an invitation for her to expand on her thoughts.

She gripped me by the suit coat that had been her lover's. She said: 'I'm just understanding. I mean about Joanou coming in that bus — coming towards this villa.'

I took hold of her hands. I said: 'You know who he is? I mean, his connections with the murder gang that Christopholou and Joanou belong to?'

'I've heard things said.' She wasn't as sure as Keremetlian. 'Lots of people hinted that Hagop Joanou's money was behind this anti-British trouble.' She seemed to grip me harder. 'Now do you realise what he is doing here?'

I wrinkled my nose. I must have been dumb. I couldn't think of anything.

I told her so. 'Honey, I just don't get a clue. You tell me.'

She didn't tell me right away. Her eyes were looking beyond me at the door. I turned quickly. It was opening slowly. She got behind me and I took hold of the handle and jerked and pulled it open.

7

Trouble's coming

Miss George came in quickly on the other side of that door handle. At once she recovered her balance. I looked down onto her untidy grey hair, onto a thin, sunken face that betrayed her age. I saw the blanket drooped around her thin, bony shoulders.

But mostly I looked at her faded grey eyes. They looked at me and then looked beyond at Charmain, and they were the picture of concentrated malevolence.

She spoke, but she didn't take her eyes away from Charmain, standing stiffly by my side. I could feel the fear pulsing through that lovely Greek's young body. She was more scared of Miss George than of anyone in that lounge, I was prepared to bet.

'I wouldn't want any harm to come to you. You're a nice boy.' It was the first time in years anyone had called me a nice boy. 'But you're bound to come to harm if you let yourself go to this woman.'

I knew what she meant. I grinned at Charmain. I drawled: 'I guess there ain't no future for us in this house, Charmain.' Then I patted Miss George on her bony shoulder and said, kindly: 'I keep telling you. I won't get caught up. Charmain's wanting to talk to me, nothing else.'

It was the truth so far as I was concerned right then. Miss George wasn't altogether reassured. She went back through that door and everyone looked at us.

Especially that old man with his young wife looked at us. I guess it burned him up, because I knew what he'd been thinking, watching us both go into that bedroom. His wife's eyes were very hard and bright, too, and she was watching us both intently, looking . . . and being disappointed.

I saw the blue-jowled Joanou's eyes upon us. They shifted away when I looked at him. I knew he was jealous, too.

I looked around and B.G. and the

Armenian were lying together like brothers, snoring.

Charmain got me down apart from the others. She wanted to tell me more, and I wanted to hear it.

Tomorrow there would be the police, and the more I knew the better it would be to help them. I'm a great guy for helping cops — when someone else has done the murder.

I said: 'What about Joanou? Why is he up here?'

She watched that fleshy man wedged into the chair that had so comfortably carried the bulk of the Armenian. I could hardly hear her words.

'Chris dropped a hint that pressure was being put on him to do another job.' Another job — it sounded like another killing. 'He was scared. He didn't want to experience again what he'd already been through. But the mob had a hold on him. They were able to threaten to expose him if he didn't go through with this second killing they were planning.'

'You think Joanou was on his way out to talk to him about this new killing?'

My eyes were on Joanou's pockets. Could be there was something heavy in one of them. Could be it was a gun.

And yet Joanou didn't look to have the guts to face a man in hiding from a murder rap.

I wondered if Joanou had other plans connected with this villa. Maybe he thought he should have inherited Charmain instead of Christopholou, I thought cynically, but I didn't pursue the thought.

I said: 'What are you getting at?'

She nodded towards Joanou. She told me something then that I hadn't suspected before. And yet it made sense of the killing of the bus driver. 'Someone, hanging out of the bus, killed Chris.' Her eyes jumped to mine. Perhaps she'd thought all along I must have known. I kept a poker face. I didn't want to betray surprise. She went on: 'You knew that, of course. No one could have been out on the road at that time of night. No one would know that Chris would be down to meet the bus. I had to ring a friend in Kyrenia to make the arrangement. But no one else would know.'

I licked my lips. The bus driver had said something about his mirror. Perhaps he had caught the flash of a gun being fired behind him. Then I remembered that right about that time I heard a bang and thought it was a tyre bursting.

I said: 'You thought another guy had done this killing. That editor man. The crazy-pants who's jealous of any man looking at you.'

She nodded. She was watching Joanou and brooding.

I said: 'Now you've shifted your suspicion. Now you're figuring it could be Joanou who killed your new boyfriend.'

The theory might have suited Charmain. But it didn't please me because I was remembering things.

The one thing that puzzled me was that it fitted in with what the Cypriot bus driver had said to me about seeing something in his mirror. That was something I'd have to work out later. If Christopholou had been killed by someone in the bus and not out on the roadway, who had done it?

Charmain was saying: 'Perhaps Joanou

really wanted Christopholou out of the way. He knew too much about the men behind these disturbances — this recent killing. Perhaps he saw his chance unexpectedly when Chris stood out there, flagging the bus.'

I said: 'Maybe.' But I was thinking: Joanou was in this lounge when I turned off the light in the kitchen and saw some guy standing out in the storm, watching us through the window.

There was a whole lot of this jigsaw that didn't fit. I thought I wouldn't try fitting the pieces together yet. I'd just stick around and then hand over the puzzle to the professionals to finish when the sun shone the following morning.

The storm was fast blowing out. It was three in the morning. In another couple of hours there'd be daylight. I got down beside the Armenian and pillowed against his round shoulder. Charmain got down beside me. She wasn't going to leave me at all that night.

When I looked up I saw Miss George's eyes on us. They were disapproving. More, they were filled with a burning

144

hatred that told me this girl wouldn't get any mercy at the hands of Miss Paterson's friend.

I wondered then if in fact Miss George hadn't been the greater sufferer by the death of George Arthur Paterson. Maybe this old duck had been in love with him. Maybe that's why she hated so much. I thought I'd keep the two women apart if I could.

Then I went to sleep . . .

Sunshine was on my face. I groaned and moved. I hoisted myself away from the Armenian and screwed my eyes against the sudden intensity of new-risen sun. Then I tried to get on to my feet and a flood of agony swept over my bruised, aching body. That floor was not at all *sympatico*.

The others were stirring, too. The warm sunshine all in a moment had dispelled the chill and gloom from the lounge. The air was bad from too many people in too small a space. I stepped over legs and went to the French window and threw it open.

I looked out onto a world that was

glorious. It was impossible to believe there had been that violent storm in the night. I saw mountains tinged with morning sunshine. Mighty slopes that stretched northwards towards a Mediterranean so blue it didn't seem real. Like a child's painting of a blue sea, I thought.

I saw the winding road descend onto that plain, and I could see the beginnings of cultivation — silver-leaved olive groves on the mountain slopes. Then denser, darker-hued citrus plantations. Then the whiteness of buildings that marked Kyrenia on a headland . . . and then that glorious strip of golden sand, and the white surf breaking on it, the green of shallow waters and then that intense blue of the sea that went out and across to distant Turkey. I saw the faint blue smudges that marked Anatolia across the water.

Everyone started to move about. I went around that villa and then came back and said there was no one to be seen. The killer had gone with the storm.

Then I went down to the bus, leaving the women to make a breakfast for us.

The bus was still there. I was horrified, seeing it in the daylight. It seemed to overhang that precipice edge to an extent greater than I had imagined. I couldn't even go to the road edge because the drop beyond was too ghastly to contemplate.

I saw the body of Christopholou wrapped around the rear wheel, and then I went quickly back to the villa and got myself a strong coffee. The two English women had made it. Charmain had been a lily again this morning, prettying herself in that bedroom and leaving the work to others.

Right after breakfast I said I was going to walk into Kyrenia. Maybe traffic would be along the road before I got back. They should send the driver on to pick me up and get the police, I told them.

It would take two hours to get there, even though the way was so abruptly downhill at first. I didn't see many volunteers for that long walk, and I didn't like the idea myself. But someone had to do it and I didn't want to hang around that villa any longer.

I asked B.G. if he wanted to come with me. He looked fatter than ever and mumbled something about not feeling up to it. But Charmain followed me down the roadway. She had attached herself to me. She hated the thought of that long walk, but much more she hated the thought of losing me as a protector.

And that was curious. Because I just didn't figure myself in that role at all.

We met a car when we were down level with the first olive trees. The Cypriot driver was obliging. Charmain spoke to him. She turned on the charm. After that he was wax in her hands, and he took us back to the police station in Kyrenia at a reckless pace. By now the sun was high and the world was very hot and uncomfortable. Already the first dust was rising from a road that had been so heavily saturated during the night.

The police took down my statement. They questioned Charmain and when they learnt her identity they looked at her in a curious manner. They weren't impressionable like that Cypriot driver. They told us we could go to an hotel but not to leave it until they had been out and investigated our report.

That suited me. I started to go to an hotel that was built on a jetty, seemingly — at any rate it was surrounded on three sides by sea. I thought it was a heavenly place. I wouldn't find a better anywhere for that long sleep I had promised myself. That was all I could think about right then, getting the ache out of my seat.

We walked together to that hotel from the police station, Charmain and I. We caused quite a bit of comment, I knew. I felt that behind me heads were turning. It wasn't usual to see a girl as lovely as Charmain walking Kyrenia's streets, with an American in a suit most obviously not designed for him.

I couldn't give a damn for what they thought, and Charmain had recovered her poise and coolness and never so much as glanced towards the interested passers-by.

I thought she had recovered her nerve, but in time I began to realise that she was as taut as a piano wire — and just as responsive. There was a lot going on in

149

that sharp mind of hers.

I said, when we were walking out towards that sea-girt hotel: 'We seem to be going the same way.'

She just looked at me. I had an uneasy thrill of apprehension with that look, and that isn't usual with Joe P. Heggy. I thought: Ugh, ugh. She's going to do a poison ivy act on you, Joseph, if you don't watch out.

Right then I began to feel I ought to start running away from this dame, just like Berny had run out on the demure but passionate little Miss Dunkley.

Then I dismissed the thought. We went into the hotel. I was big. I said: 'I'll stand you a breakfast.'

I signed myself in. Told them my grip would be along when they salvaged that bus.

I saw Charmain writing her name in the register. That made me jump again. I was beginning to think I'd become married to the girl, and I didn't want it. But it wasn't my hotel. If she wanted to put up here, that had nothing to do with me. So long as she paid her own bills.

We breakfasted. I scrambled through mine quickly, because the day was already too hot and my tiredness was intensified. I wanted to get to my bed.

I looked at Charmain often and wondered that she could look so fresh and cool and untired. She must have had as bad a night as most of us — perhaps worse.

Then B.G. and the other passengers came trooping into the hotel. That is, all except the Turkish Cypriot. But the old man with the young wife was fussily there, and Keremetlian bummed his way into the breakfast room. Joanou came in and the two English women. It was quite a party.

A relief bus had been sent out from Nicosia to look for the one stranded in the hills by the storm. They'd collected the passengers and our grips and brought, them on to Kyrenia. B.G. said they'd passed a police car coming out.

'You'll be for questioning later,' I told him. Then we moved into the reception hall. We were all looking for beds.

That old man with the young wife was

well ahead of us. He hadn't bothered about breakfast. My hunch must have been correct. Last night should have been their honeymoon night. Right now the old man was wanting to catch up on time.

His bride, almost stolidly unemotional, looked back at us over the head of her small spouse. Her eyes met mine. Perhaps she was thinking the old man had got the better of that bargain.

I went up those stairs. Charmain came a couple of steps behind me. As we came out on to the balustraded top I looked down over the ferns and palms and I saw two lonely little figures watching us from the ground floor. Miss Paterson was just watching us. But Miss George seemed to have hooks in her eyes and they were lacerating into the comely flesh of Charmain.

All I could do was to hunch my shoulders and spread out my hands as much as to say: 'What can I do about it?'

We parted outside my door. She would have lingered, I knew, but I went in after saying, laconically: 'Be seeing you, honey.'

Then I stripped off and had a shower

and then lay on top of the bed that was drenched with sun. I pulled a sheet over me and fell asleep.

Hours later I awoke. I felt good. There wasn't an ache in my body.

The sun had moved round and now my room was cool because of the shade and because of that exhilarating breeze that came whipping in from the sparkling Mediterranean below my window.

My delight left me.

I'd had a visitor while I slept. The visitor was still there. She was painting her nails.

I rolled on my side and rubbed my hair inelegantly and yawned without putting my hand to my mouth.

I growled: 'How did you get in?'

She took time off from her manicuring and nodded towards the open windows. They gave out on to a balcony. I could see that balcony ran towards an adjoining one. It wouldn't be hard for a determined girl to skip the intervening wall, I thought. And then I thought: 'I guess Charmain's mighty determined.'

Charmain didn't speak. I got to dislike

the silence and I said, firmly; 'It's kind of unusual to find dames walking in on a man while he sleeps. Some people might object.'

By rights I ought to have been objecting. All that I knew about Charmain didn't add up to her advantage. But a man just can't keep up a grouch when the girl in question is as lovely as Aphrodite, goddess of this lovely Cyprus island.

I had to work hard, in fact, to sound peevish at all. She'd changed into a dress that was plain white with cross over lapels that didn't cross until they were way down that beautiful torso of hers. The whiteness was relieved by a vivid red belt and by a little red monogram on the left lapel. It accentuated the glorious richness of that dark wavy hair of hers, and it made her face seem delightfully brown and healthy. She looked wholesome. Something clean and infinitely desirable.

She quit beating about the bush. She put away her little bottle and brush and then lifted her eyes to look at me. They were as hard as hell. I never knew anyone who got down to ways and means as boldly as Charmain.

She said: 'It's time you started to think. If you like living.'

I reached for my cigarettes. They were in my jacket pocket. And that was across the room.

I got up, that sheet draped around me, and I stalked across and got a smoke.

She watched me and there wasn't the slightest interest in her eyes. At the moment she was here on business, I thought ironically. Well, I didn't want any business relations with Charmain.

I said: 'You'd better tell me about premature deaths. I'm interested. Tell me I'm morbid, but go on, give me the details, baby.'

She came across and helped herself to a cigarette. She didn't ask for a light but deliberately put that cigarette between her red lips and then lit up from mine. It brought us very close together, and that was how she wanted it. She blew smoke, but even then didn't try to go away.

It was strictly business, but she was using all she had to gain the deal. I wouldn't move, either. I felt I had to stand up to her and not start running away. In any event I didn't run away on dames. I didn't know how.

She said: 'The Joanou mob has power on this island. They won't let you live, Joe.'

She was pushing aside that sheet, and stroking my shoulder beneath. It gave me a sensation, that caressing motion.

I said: 'Come again, honey. Why should the Joanou mob have any interest in me at all?'

She said, emptily, without the slightest trace of emotion: 'Because of me. I've been seen too much with you since Chris got killed. It won't be liked. When they know — as they will know — that we're registered in adjoining rooms in this same hotel, I think they'll do something.'

I griped: 'Why didn't you think of all this before? Goddamnit woman, why bring trouble on me?'

When I looked at her I knew the answer. She was the kind of girl who doesn't believe in inheriting all the trouble herself. She liked to spread it about a bit. She was deliberately getting me involved, and I knew why.

'You think that if I get on the run with you, we'll run together as a team, ugh? You've still got your mind on U.S. citizenship.' My voice was cynical. But I was uneasy underneath. Charmain had a way of getting what she wanted.

She was quite cool about it. 'There's no future for me in Cyprus any more. I'm too well known. I don't have a chance of living here any longer.'

She was caressing me again, and now her other hand was going behind my neck. She'd put down her cigarette in order to give me all her attention.

She said: 'I want to go to America. I've always wanted to go there, but I can't — not until some American marries me. Then I can go.'

'You got my answer before on that subject, baby. Don't make me behave like a heel and turn you down a second time.'

My sarcasm didn't affect her. 'There's no reason why you shouldn't help me. I've got plenty of money hidden away. It's yours if you make me an American citizen and get me into New York. You don't ever need to see me again, once I'm in America, and you don't need to worry about me.'

Her eyes dropped before mine. 'I know how to look after myself.'

I said: 'I bet you do, baby.'

I was liking her caresses. I didn't want her to stop now. But I couldn't say yes to her proposition. She was poison ivy all right, and I wasn't going to give in against my better judgment.

I asked: 'Tell me, why should the Joanou mob want to bump you off — and now me, too?'

She shrugged those shapely shoulders. She was mighty cool. 'You don't know Cyprus — or men like Hagop Joanou.'

Her eyes lifted to mine. 'They have a tremendous pride, and family honour is something you Americans can't understand. I told you the Joanous didn't like Yangos living with me. But when I went to Chris it seemed to them to affect their honour.' Cynically she said: 'I suppose I was expected to behave like a widow.'

I waited for her to go on. I was

understanding — a little.

Her eyes were sombre. 'I think Hagop Joanou came all the way from Nicosia to kill Christopholou. Perhaps he intended to kill me, too.' Again she shrugged. 'Things like that happen often in Cyprus. When your honour is involved you take a gun and shoot someone. Or use a knife.'

I said: 'That's a warning. I'll keep away from Cypriot womenfolk. And that goes for you, too, honey.'

She looked at me very levelly and said: 'I'm not letting you go. That's why I think the Joanou mob will try to kill you. They'll try to get rid of me because I know too much, quite apart from Hagop Joanou's personal dislike of me. They'll have to go for you because they'll think that I am certain to open my mouth to you.'

'Which you are doing, sweetheart.' My cigarette seemed suddenly to have a bad taste. I said: 'But there's one thing you overlook. You can wish yourself upon me, but that doesn't mean to say I'm going to be saddled with you. You're a fine-looking girl, Charmain, but you haven't got all that to make me want to run my head into a noose. You spell too much trouble for any man!'

She turned at that and went towards the balcony. She just said, lightly: 'Try to get rid of me.' Her eyes were mocking as she turned towards me. 'I'll be around, don't worry, Joe.'

Someone knocked on my door. Charmain whisked her shapely legs over the low parapet that divided her balcony from mine.

I went carefully to that door and opened it with my foot against the bottom. I took Charmain's warning seriously. I knew I was on the spot. A lot of murder had been committed and my life would be taken easily if the killers thought it was helping to safeguard them.

I felt jumpy at the thought. It's spine-chilling to be away from your own country and find yourself up against murder.

It was B.G. I let him in. He was in good spirits, and talked all the time I bathed and shaved and got dressed. His theme hadn't changed.

He was talking about the absent Miss Dunkley as if he had been making a mistake all along. He was giving her a mental build up, and he didn't know why he was doing it.

He said: 'She's really a wonderful little woman, Joe.' I grunted, sticking my head through a shirt. I didn't think any woman was wonderful right then. I guess Charmain had gone sour on me.

I told him bluntly: 'You're trying to talk yourself right out of Cyprus. You're trying to work up an excuse to get you back to Istanbul — and little Lav.'

He looked indignant. I ignored it. He was only the boss.

I went on: 'Okay, if that's how you want it, let's go. The heck, this island's too warm fur me.' He didn't understand. I thought I'd tell him later.

Now, the damned fool had to back pedal. No, he yapped, we wouldn't go back right away. We'd hang on a day or two and enjoy ourselves. I guess he thought it would look plain foolish if we flew back to Istanbul the day after we'd left it.

The thing was settled for us, anyway, almost immediately. I was fixing my tie, standing at my window, looking along the rugged northern coastline. The view as superb and inviting. I wasn't seeing much of it. I was wondering when someone was going to come round to try to make me a stiff. That spoils any view, thinking of the many ways you might die in the next hours.

A car pulled in at the hotel entrance below. I didn't pay much attention at first. Then I saw someone step out, someone walked resolutely towards the main doors.

I turned to B.G. 'Brother, trouble's coming. And not for me, either!'

8

One room!

We went down to meet her. B.G. was suddenly red and confused and in a panic. I made the fat slob go down. In the entrance lounge stood Lavinia. She'd followed her boy friend all the way from Istanbul. She wasn't going to let go of him, having found a man pretty late in her life.

But as I came down those steps, dragging B.G. with me, I whistled. This wasn't the Lavinia we'd left.

She'd thrown away her dowdy spinster clothes, and now she looked trim and neat and even attractive. She looked younger. B.G. sure had done her a lot of good.

I looked onto a newly-waved head of hair. On a face adorned with unaccustomed lipstick. I saw a figure, and it wasn't at all bad. I thought: B.G., you picked something better than I imagined.

Lavinia was even getting out of the habit of blushing. She knew what she wanted and she was going recklessly for it. At this moment she was as direct and unscrupulous as Charmain, I thought.

I said, cheerfully: 'Boy meets girl — again!' I managed to keep the sarcasm out of my voice.

They stood and looked at each other, not knowing what to do. I knew B.G. would bolt if he got half a chance, so I shoved him forward until she got hold of his hand, and then I knew he wasn't going to get away from her this time.

I helped matters. I said: 'Lav, honey, he's done nothing but talk about you ever since he left Istanbul. He's been telling me I don't understand you. Beats me why the sap ever ran out on you.'

The boss said something in a strangled voice. I knew it didn't matter. Lavinia had found her man.

I left them to it. I was just passing the door of the restaurant, when I saw a picture of dejection inside.

It was the little Armenian private eye.

He was sitting alone in that big dining room, and you could see he was sweating and in fear. I looked across the room and I saw stern-eyed waiters watching him, and I knew at once what it added up to.

I went across to him. I tell you, I had quite a liking for that little Armenian.

A smile of joy came to that round, red, bright face of his. He started to talk. He'd made a mistake. Would you believe it, he'd found himself short of money! I believed it. I thought he'd got a breakfast and had hoped to find a sucker to pay for it. The sucker was right there now — me.

I paid. I made a friend, then. Sometimes a friend comes in handy, but I didn't pay that bill for that reason. I didn't miss the money and he was rather a nice little man.

I pulled myself together, going out into the sunshine. I was getting sentimental. Maybe sight of those two lovebirds, B.G. and little Lav, was affecting me. I told myself to jump out of the mood. In the next few hours there would be no time for sentiment.

I went to the wall that fronted the

hotel. I felt it was safe to go so far away from the building, but I wasn't going into Kyrenia itself, no matter how nice it looked. In that sprawling little town, with its maze of back streets and narrow alleys, lots of things could happen to me. I was a stranger, too, and Joanou and his followers would be on their home ground.

I sat on the wall in the sunshine and tried to work things out. I couldn't. Everything was contradictory. The one thing I did believe was that Charmain was right, that the heat had been turned on her since yesterday and now it would include me because I'd been seen too much in her company.

I tried to make plans, but they didn't jell. I thought: I'll just stick close to this hotel for the next few days. I'll be safe enough here. I'd told the police everything I knew and now they'd be looking for Editor Haverford and that might remove one menace to my safety. But it wouldn't touch Joanou, because I hadn't said anything to the police except that he was with the passengers in the bus at the time of the Christopholou killing. After all, I'd only gossip from Charmain and Keremetlian to lay against the fellow.

I was getting sleepy, sitting out there in the sunshine. Maybe I should have stayed in bed longer that morning. Then I remembered that Charmain had wakened me by coming into my room. She wouldn't have let me go on sleeping, I knew. I wondered what she was doing now, and guessed she was prettying herself in her room . . .

I saw a man walk up along the sea road and enter my hotel. There was something familiar about him. I slid off the wall and went into the coolness of the hotel — I wanted a drink, anyway.

When I got into the reception lounge that familiar figure was just walking away from the register. I came after him. He went straight up to Charmain's room. I stood at the end of a well-carpeted corridor and watched while he knocked. Charmain opened the door cautiously. The fellow slammed his shoulder against it the moment it began to move, and then he went inside Charmain's room and I heard a bolt shoot across.

I went into my room and got onto the balcony and gained access to Charmain's room, that way. They looked in surprise at me as I entered. Charmain looked mightily pleased — Editor Haverford looked anything but.

For I knew it was Editor Haverford. I'd realised that the second I saw him coming towards the hotel. I should have known, seeing that curiously pale, pointed chin of his — that be-glassed passenger who had sat in the bus along with us the previous day . . . the English passenger who had disappeared in the storm during the night.

I understood a whole lot right then. I even thought to speak about it.

I saw Charmain start to jump towards me, her eyes wide and glad and yet apprehensive. I heard Editor Haverford shout something, and I knew he was crazy mad with jealousy. It must have confirmed a lot of things in his mind when he saw me come into the girl's room by way of the balcony.

I saw a gun in his hand and I cursed. I'd forgotten that, that he'd be armed.

But I thought of it too late. Now I couldn't go back.

I looked at his curiously white chin. I thought: 'I should have suspected. He wouldn't keep to his beard after what he did to the Joanou mob.' Aloud I said: 'I figured you'd broken your neck in the storm last night. I should have known.'

I should have known he was Editor Haverford the killer of Christopholou who had got the girl he wanted. Then I remembered. The killer, also, of that poor Cypriot bus driver.

Haverford had pitched the bus driver into space to silence him, to remove a man who knew too much.

I looked at Charmain. Her eyes were watching that gun as if fascinated by the ugly blue snout. I said: 'You should have talked more freely, Charmain. You knew Haverford had got rid of his pretty curly beard.'

The gun seemed to jump forward menacingly. Haverford was a man touchy about his dignity, evidently.

She whispered: 'I recognised him even without it . . . in Nicosia. That's why I sent word through for Chris to meet me. Haverford got on the bus, though . . . '

It was clearing up matters a little, but knowing the truth now didn't seem likely to help me. I looked at that insignificant face behind the glasses. No wonder he had grown a beard! There was nothing impressive about Peter John Haverford. I saw the strain upon that curiously small face. And I noticed the crazy gleam in his eyes back of those glasses. Editor Haverford had done too much that was bad in the last hours and he wasn't standing up to it well mentally. I decided to treat him with great caution. When a man's killed twice it's beginning to be a habit and I didn't want to be a third corpse to add to the recent total.

He almost shouted: 'Stop talking!' He was trembling. He was a wreck of a man now, but he was all the more dangerous for it. His eyes switched across to Charmain.

He began to curse her. He called her a lot of names and none of them was good. Charmain didn't mind at all. She was just scared of bullets. She had the sense to keep away from me now, because I don't suppose he could have stood for it if she had been within touching distance of me. He was off his head with jealousy.

When he'd cussed her good and plenty he turned to me again. 'You're not going to live,' he told me, his voice high-pitched and with that crazy note trembling in it.

'If you don't hold that gun more steadily, I figure you'll be right in what you say,' I said, but I didn't feel as easy as I tried to sound. I lifted my eyes to his. 'But if you do kill me, brother, I don't see you getting out of this hotel so easily. The cops are already looking for you, you know.'

He knew it. He said, that hysteria evident in his voice again: 'You tipped them off?'

I nodded. There was no sense in denying it. I'd talked about Editor Haverford, though I hadn't connected the name with one of the bus passengers.

He said abruptly: 'You're both going with me.' He licked his lips and that gun came up and it was covering me and not Charmain now. 'You're going to die, American.'

'And me?' That was Charmain. Bless her, she was thinking of herself again.

I saw that sap trembling. His eyes were pitiful and beseeching. He said in a whisper: 'Maybe I'll kill you, too. It depends how nice you are to me. Perhaps then I'll kill myself. I can't live without you, Charmain, but I don't think I want you after you've been with other men.'

His glance came back to me quickly and I thought I was going to get a bullet right then and there. His rage drove away his self-pity and he was in a fury as he thought of me enjoying what Charmain had possibly denied him.

I licked my lips now, looking at that vicious little automatic. I protested: 'You've got me wrong, brother. I have been trying to keep a good distance between me and your girl friend. She'll tell you the same.'

He said: 'That's a lie. You were enjoying yourselves in the kitchen back there.' His head jerked, indicating the villa in the mountains. 'And I saw you together in the bedroom.'

I shrugged. He'd go on believing what

he wanted to believe, though it was sheer hell for him to believe it.

I said: 'All right, have it your own way. Now what?' I felt truculent in spite of that gun. I wanted to reach out and knock some sense into his woman-crazed brain.

But I didn't move. I knew that trigger-finger could beat me if I went to attack him.

He jerked his gun, indicating the door. He said: 'You go out. You two keep together right in front of me. I'm desperate, remember. One false move from either of you and all three of us die.'

I knew he meant it. He was near to the end of his mental tether, and he was probably looking for an excuse to remove me and even Charmain, and then stop this awful torment that was within himself.

I moved across the carpeted floor forwards the door. Charmain came behind me. We both walked without taking our eyes off that gun. I was just going to turn the door handle when I heard a knock.

It was so loud in the silence of that

corridor that I thought for a moment it was on the door of Charmain's room. Then I realised it was a couple of yards down the corridor. It was a knock on my door.

We all halted, undecided what to do. I heard that knock again. And then I heard a voice and it was familiar.

'You don't need to be afraid, Mr. Heggy. It's me, Keremetlian, the private eye.'

A pause. The Armenian must have got tired. He knocked again and now he called: 'I found my money. You wouldn't believe where it was. I'd put it in my shoe for safety. I want to pay you back for that breakfast.'

I found myself straightening and even smiling a little, hearing that naive voice out in the corridor. Keremetlian was an honest guy, after all. I'd misjudged him. He had lost his money, temporarily.

But we couldn't go out in the corridor. I knew better than to try with that gun only a couple of feet from my spinal column.

We waited. The Armenian hammered

once again and then must have decided I wasn't holding out on him but was genuinely out. We heard him grumble and walk away. Five minutes later Haverford told me to open the door.

We walked down the corridor, Charmain and I together, and Editor Haverford stepping on our heels. I didn't look behind, but knowing my movies I guessed that gun would be in his jacket pocket and pointing at us through the material. It was just as deadly.

We walked down the broad, shallow, carpeted stairs. All the time I was looking for people, hoping someone would come across and speak to us. I thought it might give us a chance, though a slim chance, of turning the tables on this thin-faced, washed-up ex-newspaper editor.

That hotel seemed astonishingly deserted. When I wanted them I couldn't see anyone I knew.

We went out into the sunshine. There was a car parked to our right. I heard Haverford say: 'We'll take that car. You drive, American.'

We were walking towards the car when

I heard a yell in the distance. I looked towards the sea wall. The Armenian was just jumping down. We got to the car. I looked over the roof. The Armenian was getting his feet into his shoes. I knew he'd never win the race.

Haverford shoved us into the car. Me behind the wheel. Charmain by my side where he could cover us both. And he sat on the rear seat, that gun nakedly exposed now.

He said: 'Drive — drive out of the town and into the hills!'

I started up and went out towards the town. I had a momentary picture in my mirror of Keremetlian standing and staring after us as we drove away. I felt my last chance had gone.

Being taken for a ride was something I understood, coming from America. I also knew that a man rarely came back from a ride in one piece. With his hands full of steering wheel, I reckon a guy is at a disadvantage with a gun pressed into his back. That's how I felt, threading my way through an unfamiliar town.

I didn't know where I was going.

Haverford might have known but he didn't care. All he wanted was to get us both out into the wilds of that mountain range.

We were still travelling along the coast road, when we got through Kyrenia, and he shouted for me to take the first turn to the right. I did and we went bumping up a poor road that led into the mountains.

It was getting late in the afternoon. The sun was down behind us, and it worried me in the mirror. I kept my head away so that I didn't keep getting the reflection in my eyes. Then, nearly an hour's run later into the hills, I automatically glanced into that mirror.

My heart jumped. A car was following only a quarter of a mile behind us.

Haverford didn't suspect, I knew.

He was sitting in the back of the car in some sort of trance. I guess the poor devil was going through hell, planning what he was planning.

It can't be easy, to contemplate killing a man and then perhaps kill the woman he was crazy about. And that was in his mind, both Charmain and I knew.

Charmain and I, in any event, didn't feel so good, either, sitting there in front of that crazy killer with the dead white chin.

I got a glimpse of a black car gaining on us. I saw to it that it did gain. I played cunning and took my time at the corners, and I only hoped that Haverford wouldn't look behind and see that overtaking sedan.

We went through a couple of hill villages. I thought of stopping, but I realised Haverford would put a bullet into both of us and then turn the gun on himself without any hesitation. I kept going. I was trying to make plans, and they concerned that following car.

It was very near behind us now. The light wasn't too good, because nights come swiftly upon sunset in Cyprus. I nudged with my knee, because I could guess how Charmain was feeling. When I felt her eyes steal round to look at me I glanced significantly up at my driving mirror.

She had sense. She began to manoeuvre so that she could look into it. I drove on, taking it easily. We seemed to have left the last of the villages behind. Ahead were tremendous mountains, bare except for where afforestation schemes had been instituted.

Suddenly I saw that that following car was only a hundred yards behind us. It seemed pretty well packed, in the way of Cypriot cars. It pleased me, to see all those people. We might need them in a minute. I was thinking of standing on the brakes suddenly, and rolling out through the doorway at the same time . . .

Charmain suddenly screamed. It was a shout, but it was so high-pitched and frightened I rated it in the scream class. She grabbed my arm.

Dimly I understood what she was saying. She was telling me to step on it.

That following car contained the Joanou mob!

It startled Haverford, too. I looked in the mirror and saw him whirl and face back through a rear window. It would have been my chance to have rolled out of the car except for that following menace. I wasn't rolling out of any car with the

Joanou mob right behind us.

I tried to shove my foot clean through the floorboards. We entered a long climbing valley at a pace that was just plain crazy. That sedan came rocketing behind just as crazily.

Haverford was shouting: 'Faster, faster! If they catch up with us we'll all be done in!' I couldn't see his point of view. He was intending us all to be done in anyway, wasn't he?

But I hadn't any intention of quitting this life that night if I could help it. I drove, and I drove so well that I made distance between me and that sedan. Ironically I heard Haverford encouraging me, complimenting me.

He'd tried to lean out of the window to fire at the sedan following, but his aim must have been yards wide of the mark in that bumping, lurching vehicle on a road designed for nothing better than ox carts.

I found our car was gradually leaving the other behind. I began to wonder about that. What in heck's name was the good of outdistancing those Joanou thugs if it left us at the mercy of Haverford again?

I made my decisions. I had to take risks. I got my hand down and gripped Charmain's arm quickly and hoped she understood that I was about to do something reckless.

We were running through another afforestation area. The dark pines reared in geometrical patterns to our left. On our right the road fell steeply and was bare for a few hundred yards until more level ground permitted further tree planting.

Haverford was shouting in triumph on the rear seat. He was waving his gun and I thought he was more cuckoo than ever.

I did a whole lot of things all at once. I leaned across Charmain and pulled her towards me and opened the door at my side. In the same movement I stood on the brakes and turned the steering wheel and headed the car over the edge of the road.

As it began to jump into space, Charmain and I fell out through my open doorway on to the road. We heard Haverford begin to scream. We couldn't do anything about that.

We got to our feet and risked one quick glance down that slope. The car was still sailing through the air. As we looked it came down on all four wheels and then seemed to bounce in among the treetops. There was an almighty crashing sound as trees gave before that weight. We didn't wait to see any more.

I grabbed Charmain and pulled her up the far bank and then began to drag her among the trees. We heard the Joanou car come skidding to a halt. They'd seen the wreckage over the road edge. I was praying they would go on looking at it and give us a chance to get away into the hills. These trees offered good cover and within half an hour there would be darkness and then no one would be able to find us there.

Charmain came on gallantly. She might have shunned exertion at a normal time, but with her pretty neck at stake she made no complaints and legged it along almost as fast as I could.

A shout behind told us we had been seen. One of the mob must have glanced round and caught a movement as we struggled through the trees a hundred yards away. They began to come after us.

We went climbing up that hill, dodging about among the trees so as not to get sighted along an avenue, and our tortured lungs began to glow red hot. That climb was murder.

Charmain packed in after a time. She just wasn't made for mountaineering. I should have left her, because she was no good and I had no feeling for her. But, somehow a man can't run away from a woman who he knows will go under if she is caught.

I grabbed Charmain's wrist and dragged her along, though her breath was sobbing and she was moaning with the exertion. I'd no breath to say anything to her myself. Perspiration was blinding me. I just went on struggling upwards, hearing the sounds of men's heavy forms crashing through the undergrowth behind us.

It was a nightmare, trying to keep ahead of those pursuers until night came to shelter us. Twice they got a sight on us and guns boomed off. They did boom, too, and I knew they were sporting guns and not rifles. But they could kill at close range and even cripple at a distance.

We must have been very lucky, because though I heard lead smacking into tree trunks about us, nothing hit us.

It was getting darker. Another five minutes and they wouldn't be able to find us, I kept telling myself.

Then I ran onto one of them. I don't know how I did it. Maybe he was good at anticipation, and he'd gone trekking over the shoulder of the hill and got right in front of us. We came out of those trees suddenly, on top of the hill, and I saw him only a few yards below us on the other side, crawling on hands and knees up a rain gully.

I let go of Charmain and took off in a sprawling dive that landed me flat on top of him. I knew I couldn't afford to give him a chance to get that gun up. I saw his face, a pale oval in the near-darkness, and I saw the whites of his eyes, startled as he saw me come hurtling down upon him. I'd just beaten him by a second, I knew.

My weight crashed into him. He

couldn't have been feeling any better than I. He went over and fell away from me and his gun rattled out of his hand.

I couldn't follow him. That fall had knocked the wind out of my body. I could only lie and pant and look at him, and he could only lie there and pant and look at me. And between us was that gun, and behind us we could hear the sounds of pursuit.

Charmain was on her knees, her head drooping, her chest heaving. She couldn't move, couldn't do a thing to help us.

It was up to me.

I began to crawl towards that gun, and it was the biggest effort of my life, following that awful climb. I saw the panic come into that Cypriot's face, and somehow he found the strength to roll over on to his hands and knees and he began to crawl up towards that gun.

We both started slowly, and then our pace accelerated as we realised that the loser in this race probably wouldn't live to see another sunrise.

We went on hands and knees and then suddenly, simultaneously, both of us dived forward to grab the gun. Our hands reached it at the same time. We came up together, snarling and gasping and trying to swear at each other. I saw a face close to mine, a face wet with perspiration that ran off the man's chin. I only wished it had been Hagop Joanou.

I pulled a trick on him. He was fighting tenaciously to keep that rifle, and he expected me to fight equally desperately to take it off him.

Suddenly I stopped trying to pull that gun away from him and instead I slammed it back into his arms as hard as I could. It was unexpected. He went teetering backwards, and then his heel caught and he did a slow somersault and went into space. He fell about twenty feet down the steep sloping hillside, and then his body bounced into space again and he crashed another twenty feet or so. He was still bouncing down that hillside when I grabbed Charmain by the hand and started to pull her down that rain gully. It offered some protection, at least.

The Joanou mob came over the hill, then. We heard them. We heard their gasping voices. And then one of them shouted hoarsely. Charmain sobbed and I knew that our pursuers had guessed where we had gone. I kept going as fast as I could, dragging the girl behind me. It was rough going and we stumbled frequently. Once she stumbled and went down and couldn't get up.

I went back to her, having lost my hold on her wrist. It was almost black darkness now. Any minute and we could find safety from our pursuers. I could have found it for myself easily, but I just wouldn't leave Charmain. I dragged her onto my shoulder. It was the fireman's lift, and it's pretty painful if you don't get them right on your shoulder.

I knew she wasn't comfortable and she was moaning and feebly struggling. Her legs kicked and I had to hold them together, but I kept her on my shoulder and went staggering down that gully.

Then I couldn't go any farther, I just fell into a hollow by the side of the gully and we rolled together, our arms clutching each other. We heard the gunmen come stumbling nearer. Then we saw them. Just. It was as dark as all that.

We were both trying not to breathe, I knew, but it was impossible to stop the labourings of our tortured lungs. I guessed the only thing that saved us was the noise their lungs made, the hard-pressed Joanou mob's.

They seemed right on top of us. We were lying there, without any cover except for the darkness of the night. And they almost stumbled on us, but didn't quite.

For an agonising time they seemed to hesitate just where we lay, and then they stumbled down past us and we heard their receding footsteps, and never was there a more welcome sound.

We lay there and night fell completely upon us and we knew we were safe. We were holding each other, I realised, and we didn't move long after our strained lungs had gone back to their normal rhythm. We were content to go on lying there in the darkness together. There was no need to move, anyway.

And yet we did move. In time we realised it was cold so high up in the mountains. We couldn't stay there all night. Stiffly we pulled ourselves to our feet and got our cold muscles moving again as we crawled down that mountain-side.

It wasn't pleasant work, because we didn't know what lay ahead of us and all the time we expected to break our necks down some steep drop.

Then we must have moved round the corner of a hill, for we saw lights ahead and not too far ahead, either. Almost at the same time we struggled through prickly pears and got onto a sandy, rocky road. I had a feeling that all our troubles were over.

We walked down that road hand in hand together. It seemed the most suitable way to walk in the darkness. I'd forgotten that my companion was poison to her men friends. All I knew was we were comrades surviving a common peril. And we had survived it. We'd ditched a crazy killer and dodged a pack of equally ruthless hunters!

It was easier, following that road, because it showed up as a pale ribbon of grey light in the surrounding gloom. It became easier, too, as we approached that village. When we were on the outskirts, where the low, flat-topped dwellings were in silhouette against a starry sky, I halted.

Now we were pleasantly warm. In fact I was sweating again. It was a delightful night and I didn't want to spoil it. I was thinking that maybe the Joanou mob had got into this village ahead of us.

Charmain didn't think so. She thought they'd tour back round the base of the hill and get to their car. We didn't take any risks, though.

We crept together into the first shadows of those old buildings and then we found a dark corner and we both melted into it. We stood there and watched, and my arms were about the girl. There seems no other way of standing close to a girl in shadows except that you put your arms about her. In time I realised that she was deliberately getting closer to me. She liked being held by a man, and it was putting ideas into her head again. Not that they were ever very far away.

We looked out onto the usual Cypriot village. Low buildings, many of them made of mud. An open space that was a threshing ground in daylight. A few goats and sheep penned in one corner. Thorn bushes and prickly pear growing right into the village. And only one source of light.

The houses were all in darkness. Lights aren't needed unless you're wanting to read or sew or work. Cypriots work hard during the day and don't go in for much reading at night. They were sitting in their doorways relaxing in the cool of the evening and enjoying their leisure. Some children were playing around in the dirt.

The source of light was from the inevitable open-air café. It was a small hut with a thatched extension roof in front of it. Chairs and tables were set out on the hard-packed earth floor and lordly Cypriot males were enjoying their *ouzo* or *Commandaria*. It was an all-male patronage at that bar. You don't find women in these village bars ever.

It looked a peaceful scene and we never saw anything to make us suspicious. All the men we saw were the baggy-trousered peasant type and we knew none of these would be Joanou's town-mobsters.

But we watched for a good half-hour before coming out from hiding. That half-hour must have given Charmain ideas — and plans. It upset some of my inhibitions, too.

At length I said: 'Let's go. I don't see any danger.'

We came out of those shadows together. I was holding Charmain's hand, and I heard her say: 'We'll have to stay in this village for the night. We can't get out of these mountains even if we walk all night.'

I nodded, agreeing. I didn't intend to go walking down any more mountain trails during these hours of darkness. I'd stay in this village as she suggested.

We caused a commotion, walking into the circle of light cast from that café. They hadn't expected to see us — to see a lovely town-girl and an American, both rather the worse for wear.

Children came crowding round and they brought a few dogs and pet goats with them. The women stood back a distance but watched and never missed a thing. Then the menfolk roused themselves at the bar and came out to look at us.

Charmain started to talk in Greek. The noise subsided as they listened to her. I guessed she was asking for accommodation for the night.

When she'd finished there was a lot of talking, with everyone looking at each other and seeming to argue. And then a man stepped forward, his face black with stubble so that he didn't look very prepossessing. I watched him carefully.

Charmain listened to him and then turned to me. She said: 'We're all right. This man has a room which we can have for the night.'

I was going to say: 'I don't know whether I trust this bird,' and then my mind switched to what she had said.

I rapped: 'A room? One room?'

Charmain nodded. I caught a pleased expression on her face and I knew that that was all she had asked for.

One room.

9

Manhunt

I'd got the jitters, I reckon. I was remembering that men didn't live long with Charmain, lovely though she was. Even Haverford, the editor who had aspired to her favours, was probably lying with a broken neck right now.

But there was more to my uneasiness than just that. I knew these Cypriot hill-people were Oriental in their views on womenfolk — their womenfolk. They didn't take to looseness, and they were especially tough if they thought a foreigner was playing around with one of their girls.

I'd looked at those men around me and I saw their eyes gaze hungrily on that fine figure that was Charmain's fortune. I caught the glisten of desire in them and I knew that when men want and can't have they get to being angry, and they do wild things.

I wasn't sure it was going to be an uneventful night, staying in the same room as Charmain. But she was walking after that baggy-trousered Cypriot and there was nothing I could do except follow.

It was a single room in a small wooden hut to one side of the main mass of buildings. A lamp was lit for us and we saw that the roof was thatched and the walls unfinished, and it was the crudest kind of cabin. There was no door and no windows, either.

But there was a bed. It was a wooden frame set on legs with a rope mattress. The old man brought us a straw-filled palliasse, and it looked clean, and I didn't think there would be much wrong with it. Then he went.

Charmain looked at me and the light accentuated the full roundness of her cheekbones and threw shadows. It made her face look bolder, and yet it had a softening effect and she looked more and more desirable. She didn't drop her eyes now. This was one time she could hold her own with any man.

I was smoking and I let my eyes drop from that lovely face to her young body, which showed to advantage in that summer dress. I smoked harder. I tried to think of all the men who had died for this girl. I couldn't.

Charmain said, softly: 'Well, Joe?'

I rubbed my nose. 'You know what's in my mind, of course.' I met her eyes levelly now. 'If I could get the hell away from you I would.'

She wasn't offended. She was unbuttoning her dress. She smiled. 'But you can't get away from me, Joe.'

'Not tonight,' I agreed.

I looked through that doorway. The place was kind of public, I thought. I knew I wasn't going to run away, all the same. Poison ivy or not, no man could turn away from such a moment.

When I brought my head round, she was going across to that bed, and all the way she was watching me over her shoulder.

I put out the light.

★ ★ ★

A car backfired in the night. That was hours later, when dawn was closer at hand. It could have been miles away, but sound travels clearly in those still mountains.

I sat up at once. Charmain stirred in her sleep.

I didn't move, but leaned up on my elbow, facing that rectangle of light that was the door. I went on listening.

Charmain put her arms right round me and pressed her cheek against my chest.

Then I heard the sound of an engine purring and I knew I hadn't made a mistake.

I got up so quickly I nearly threw Charmain out of the bed. I grabbed my clothes and climbed into them faster than I had done for a long time. Charmain swung her long slim legs over the edge of the bed. She began to dress. I didn't give her time to finish.

I said: 'That's the Joanou mob returning!' It could only be the Joanou mob out at that time of night. And I thought: They know we're in these hills. They guess we've found a village somewhere.

All night they must have been touring the villages, asking questions and searching. Now their search had brought them to this village, to our refuge for the night.

I dragged Charmain out of that hut before she had finished dressing. She came running with me, holding her dress in her hand. I had a sudden thought. We must have looked like the newspaper funnies, where guys are forever running around with dames not able to find time to get into their dresses.

And then the humour left me. This was too deadly a matter for fun.

We ran quickly and quietly round the back of the hut. There was still no movement and we couldn't see and we stumbled a lot and got scratched when we blundered into a patch of camel thorn. It brought me up short. For a moment we thought we were fenced in.

That car purred into the village. Then we heard a door slam, and men were talking. Their voices were controlled, subdued, but they carried easily in that still night. I whispered: 'What are they saying?'

Charmain whispered back: 'They're asking about us. They've got someone out of bed.'

I didn't have any illusions. Charmain had paid for this hut, but not everyone in the village had received money from us. A lot of glad voices would be eager to tell where the American and his girl friend were resting.

I also thought that the Joanou mob would have plenty of sympathisers in this and every village in Cyprus.

I began to go round that thorn scrub, ignoring the sharp points that dragged at my clothes and scratched into my flesh. I protected Charmain as well as I could and somehow we got through them and found ourselves in the darkness on rocky ground beyond. Charmain didn't know where to go.

But I did. I'd got it all worked out in those few seconds since we'd left the hut. It was no good trying to get anywhere off the road. It was too dark and the hazards too great. And similarly it was no good trying to escape back up the trail, because in time that would find us cornered on

199

top of the mountain. Our only chance was to circle round the village and trek down the road the way that car had come.

I figured it wouldn't be expected; it would be the last place they would think of watching, that road they had just come in by.

I said to Charmain: 'We've got to get out of these hills. I guess there's no safety for us outside the towns. It's Kyrenia or bust, honey.'

She didn't say anything. She had struggled into her dress and now she was wearing it open down the front like a housecoat. I could just see her in that gloom.

I took her hand. We went round those huts, keeping to the shadows. A blasted dog came sniffing after us, and then it got some more attractive scent and paused to investigate it and that got us out of distance.

We blundered through more prickly pears, and then we saw the faint ribbon that was the curving roadway. Thankfully we got onto it and began to hurry downhill. We could see that village over our shoulders, a bare sixty or seventy yards behind us. The car was standing without headlights, but the rear light glowed redly. We could hear the murmur of voices.

They'd be moving into position to surround that hut and capture us. I wondered what they would do then.

But we weren't in that hut. We were running as fast as we could away from that dangerous village, and it might be a long time before they realised which way we had gone. This darkness was again our friend.

I wondered how long it would be dark. While I was wondering a cock began to crow. For a second I thought: Dawn's not far off, and then I remembered that was an old theory, discarded by practice. Cocks crowed all hours of the night, as any suburban dweller can testify. Maybe we had several hours before the sun came up and revealed us to our enemies.

We stumbled along for about an hour. Charmain's shoes gave out because they weren't designed for the rough treatment they'd received. After that she had to go more slowly and it became increasingly painful for her. Then finally she was too exhausted to keep going, so I called a halt.

We sat off the roadside together, crouched between two sharp rocks. At first we were warm from the exertions of the trail, but in a few minutes we were made to realise that we were still at a height and there was a little wind stealing over the hillside that we hadn't noticed back in the hut, for instance. But here it sought us out and we were chilled and shivering. We got together, then, with our arms around each other. It was purely instinctive, the thing any couple would have done, but it didn't get us warm.

After a time our muscles grew so cold and stiff that we had to get back on to the road again. I was glad the car hadn't passed us. No doubt the Joanou mob had decided to make a thorough search of the vicinity of that village which had sheltered us during the early part of the night.

I thought: Let 'em keep searching. Meanwhile we must get out, of these hills.

We blundered on to another village. We

didn't realise we were actually in the village until dark walls rose on either side of the roadway. Then there was a sudden frightening scurry as a disturbed chicken lost its head and bolted, and a dog barked and then a lot more joined in the chorus.

They wakened the watcher. A man lurched from the shadows right in front of us. I knew as soon as I saw the starlight gleaming on a gun barrel that he was no casual sleeper-out. He was a man posted by the Joanou mob to watch for us.

I reckon he was more startled than we were. He'd never figured on us turning up there in the night, in spite of what Joanou had told him.

But we were there. He had to do something about it. I saw a hazy blur of a face that was opening to shout a warning. His left hand was reaching for the strap that supported his gun over his shoulder. It was coming off his shoulder, coming down to level and cover us.

I jumped away from Charmain. It was the only thing I could do. I knocked the gun flying from his hand and it struck sparks in the darkness. Then I swung and my fist jarred against his jaw. He went down and started to scramble away in panic. He was shouting and there was pain along with the fear in his voice. The dogs were all around us in a snapping, snarling, excited throng. The din was terrific. No one was going to sleep through that.

I grabbed Charmain again and in spite of her bare feet ran her clean through that village. I had an idea the watcher didn't see us go, either.

People were stirring. We heard men grunting and shouting inside the darkened hovels, and a baby wailed and children at once began to cry.

But we were through that village and following the trail down the mountainside.

The uproar faded in time and the last dog left us and went back to its home. I slackened pace so that we went at a walk. Charmain was wincing as her tender feet hit the rough, rocky road. I put my arm round her and supported her as best I could. I felt sorry for the girl. She must have been suffering terribly.

We rested again, and then again went on. When we resumed I said: 'That looks bad for us.'

Her tired voice asked: 'What does? Isn't everything bad tonight?' She was getting dramatic in the way of overwrought women.

I let her have the truth because it didn't help to keep her in ignorance. 'Looks like they've toured the hill villages and posted men to keep a watch out for us. My guess is there isn't a village on this mountain that hasn't been alerted for us.'

'That means — ?'

'We'd better keep away from any more villages.'

I didn't know how we were going to do that and get down on to the plain that led to Kyrenia — and safety. But obviously we couldn't walk into villages waiting to receive us. 'Something else, too.'

'Tell me. If it's bad news, it won't make any difference.' She was mighty sore, walking gingerly on her tender feet along that rough, darkened road.

'My guess is they'll have sent someone up the road after that car. We'll have them down here after us in no time.'

We kept on walking. There wasn't anything else we could do. The sky in the east was beginning to pale now.

No cock crowed at all. Obviously it must be dawn.

We walked carefully now, stopping to listen, because we didn't want to run into another village. This time we mightn't get away so easily. Anyway, it was on the cards there'd be people stirring in any village we came to now. Cypriots are early risers.

We'd halted one such time and were listening when I heard a sound behind us. My head came round. Charmain shrank against me in fear. We knew what that sound meant — the most ominous sound we could hear.

Simultaneously a bright light fell full upon us. We were looking into the headlights of an approaching car.

I whisked Charmain off the road and we crouched behind the inevitable clump of prickly pears.

I guessed we hadn't been seen. Those headlights had been a good distance behind us and though they were bright to us we must have been at the limit of their range.

We listened and heard the crescendo of sound as the car came down the hill. It was moving at quite a pace, and it burned a lot of rubber when it tyred round the corners. When I heard that urgent sound I began to understand Joanou's tactics.

The lights blazed up, we heard noise, and then there was a rush of wind and dust came swirling on to us where we crouched. And then that car was a receding red light down that winding mountain trail.

I pulled Charmain back on to the road. We started to walk after that car. It was still the only direction we could follow in the darkness. As I'd said before, it was Kyrenia or bust for us.

I told her: 'You know why they were going so fast?' She didn't say anything. She was too tired, I guess. So I told her my suspicion.

'They want to get below us along this trail. They want to be across our escape route when we come out of the mountains.'

My mind thought uneasily of what could be awaiting us when dawn came. The Joanou mob might have all their sympathisers out from the villages watching that bare mountainside for us.

It decided me.

The light was growing now and in a matter of twenty minutes or so dawn would he fully upon us. But for the moment there was still cover for our movements.

I sniffed the air. My guess was pretty good, I thought. I got a smell of pine trees in my nostrils.

I said to Charmain: 'You've got to keep going a bit longer now, honey. We've got to find those forests and lie up in them during the daylight hours. We won't live if we stick out on this open mountainside once the sun's up.'

She moaned. She'd lost both her shoes by now and her stockings were worn right off the soles of her feet. They were curling above her insteps and around her ankles. And her feet were bleeding.

But there was no time for delay. There was a half-light at the moment and the brightness was increasing rapidly.

I pulled her off the trail and now it grew more rocky and difficult to climb. We started up a stony ascent. I'd got a hunch that over the shoulder of this hill we'd find those new forests that were dotted everywhere over Cyprus. I hoped so. Within those trees we might find shelter. Outside of them, on the open slopes there'd be none.

We were a long way from the trees when daylight came fully upon us. In just a few minutes that half-light changed to full daylight as the sun's first rays climbed over the rugged eastern peaks. Ahead of us was a dark fence of fir trees.

We began to stumble more quickly towards them. We felt naked, there on that bare hillside exposed by the daylight.

Charmain was sobbing, but somehow she found the strength to continue that stumbling run right until we were in among those sweet-smelling trees. Then she collapsed. I straightened her and made her more comfortable and then went back to the entrance of the forest. I looked out.

I saw an immense valley, with patches of trees along both slopes. A road climbed up from a village about four miles away. I could just see it, a huddle of buildings that looked white in the light of the early morning sun.

Then I saw men. A group of them were across the trail only a half-mile or so away. A light caught my eye and I guessed that a car was pulled in among some bushes off that trail. That told me who those men were.

I went back to Charmain. She was in a bad way. Neither of us had eaten since the previous afternoon, and the only drink we'd had had been in that hut at the village where we'd rested during the night.

Now a tremendous thirst was upon us, and I knew it would grow intolerable as the heat of the day mounted with that climbing sun.

I looked around but I knew it was hopeless. You don't find water running in streams and wells and springs in Cyprus, not often, anyway. But we had to find water, as well as refuge.

I wiped the perspiration off Charmain's face. She was lying there, her eyes closed and her face pale with exhaustion. She wasn't my kind of girl, but she had my sympathy then. I felt sorry for her, and I told her so.

I lifted her head and shoulders and sat under them so that she was pillowed on my lap. I told her to keep on resting. We weren't in a hurry any longer, I said.

I didn't tell her about the men who blocked the road that led down towards the safety of Kyrenia. And I didn't tell her that from where they stood they could see clean across the hillside, so that if we moved from the shelter of these trees we'd be seen immediately.

The miracle was that we hadn't been detected during those few minutes while we ran towards the forest. I pushed back that lovely black hair with my fingers and tried to put a bit of spirit into the girl. I told her we'd move soon and go on and find water. She wasn't to be kidded. She knew Cyprus better than I did.

211

Her eyes opened. They were very close to mine. They still looked lovely in spite of the strain and fear lurking in them. Big, soft brown eyes that had led more than one man to madness.

She reached for my hand with her own. The red talons had been broken off in the scramble up the hillside. There was dirt on her fingers and a trace of blood where she had sustained a cut. Her dress had suffered and when I looked at her feet they were a mess.

I felt my hand gripped. Then she managed a smile.

She said: 'You're quite a guy, Joe.'

It made my head jerk up, hearing that whispered voice. There was something unusual about it. I pondered for a moment and then got it. There was a human quality in it now. As if Charmain was indulging in an emotion foreign to her. There was admiration in her eyes and gratitude, and I wondered if they had ever been there before.

She put up her hand to stroke my cheek. This night must have been shattering to have made her like this,

212

thoughtful and almost tender. It wasn't the Charmain I'd known up to now.

She met my eyes frankly. Her strength was coming back with resting. She said: 'I'd like you to like me, Joe.'

I patted her shoulder, big man style. Said: 'I like you, Charmain. There's a lot about you that any man could like.' I didn't go into details.

She shook her head. She wasn't deceived. She said:

'Why don't you take to me, Joe? I know you don't. Is it because I've loved other men?'

I shook my head. I was looking down those straight avenues of trees. It was cool under them, but there was no other comfort.

I said, truthfully: 'Nope. That isn't it. I've known girls before who've had their lovers, and I liked them. I didn't hold that against them. I can't talk, anyway.'

'Then what is it?'

I sought refuge again in looking down among those trees. The truth was that she was callous, shallow, selfish, prepared to use her beauty to gain her own end no matter how much it hurt others in the end. But I wasn't going to say that to her then.

I heard her say, softly: 'You don't need to tell me, Joe.'

I looked down. There were tears wetting those long, dark, curling eyelashes. She jerked her head away so that I wouldn't see. Her mouth seemed to writhe a little as if in some mental anguish. I cradled her more gently in my arms, sorry for her. Wanting to help her.

I said: 'Don't get het up, honey. Just relax and leave it to Uncle Joe.'

She relaxed all right. But she said: 'Joe, I'd give all that I've done in the past if I could win you. You're quite a man to have around when there's trouble.'

I guessed it was as high a compliment as ever I could hope to get. She lifted her head then, and I knew she wanted to be kissed. And then we lay there a long time and rested and the sun came overhead and dappled us with warm moving patterns.

When our thirst was intolerable we moved. She took off her stockings and wrapped them round her feet like bandages. Then I put my arm around her and we walked off, she limping badly.

We hit a trail within a quarter of a mile. That would be the trail watched over by the Joanou mob. We halted then, not knowing what to do. We were at quite a height here, because the trail came climbing up from the lower part of the valley. I looked back and it seemed as though the trail were completely deserted. I thought perhaps the Joanou mob had moved off to another position.

I said: 'It's no good going back up this trail. We're bound to run into trouble that way because it must end somewhere in the mountains. The way for us is that way.' I nodded back to where I'd seen the Joanou mob.

But I didn't move, knowing that. Because we couldn't see how we could get past that village I'd seen, out on the bare plain below the forest area. It was all right knowing where to go but it was another thing to know how to get there.

While we were trying to make up our minds, a Cypriot shepherd came into

215

view. He had a blue rag round his head and he had a long moustache and stubbly beard on his chin. And he wore the inevitable long leather boots and baggy black pants.

He shouldn't have been in that forest area and he came up the trail in a hurry, wanting to get through to pastures beyond. He was shouting and throwing stones at his flock to keep them on the move, and they were walking in several lines, nose to tail. Some were goats but most were the fat-tailed sheep that are a feature of Cyprus livestock.

I said to Charmain: 'Maybe that guy's got drink on him.'

She whispered tiredly, lying alongside me: 'He'll go back and tell.'

I shrugged. We had to get drink. I started to walk out towards him. He saw me and came to a halt, leaning on his tall stick. I saw eyes that grew suddenly frightened and I knew he'd heard of the fugitives and knew how badly they were wanted by the Joanou mob. But I was up to him before he could decide to run away, I guess.

I saluted him and gave the Greek greeting for good morning. He responded. Then I realised I knew hardly any more Greek. I was looking at his belt. He had a water bottle there, a distended bladder that undoubtedly contained liquid.

I pointed to it and brought out some Cyprus piastres.

He came across with that drink in record time. I must have made a mistake in handing out that bunch of money. I said: 'Thank you,' in Greek and then walked back to where I'd left Charmain.

I dropped on my knees beside her but she was looking beyond me. The Cypriot had changed his mind about going farther into the mountains, and now he was heading hell for leather back the way he'd come with his precious flock.

I poured water down Charmain's throat. Then I drank myself. That water was sour and tasted unpleasant because of that warm bladder container, but it was miraculous in the way it revived us. We drank it all between us and then we felt that we could stand up and fight again.

We had hardly finished that water when

we heard the shepherd shouting and waving. He wasn't waving to us. We saw the distant speck with his sheep and goats, and then we saw even smaller specks move as if in slow motion across the dry yellow valley bottom to meet him. There must have been a couple of dozen men in that group.

Charmain's face blanched. My own probably registered horror.

The Joanou mob must have turned out a whole village, and now they knew fairly accurately where to find us.

The manhunt was on in earnest. It didn't feel good at all.

I was the man.

10

If you'd been a good girl...

We started to walk back among the trees.
There was no sense in running. We
couldn't run for more than a few yards,
anyway, and even walking away from
those clamorous-voiced searchers seemed
a waste of time.

But instinct kept us walking, kept us
climbing up through those straight rows
of trees away from that dangerous trail. I
was in the lead again, towing poor
Charmain. She came on gallantly. I'd got
a greater respect for her in the last hours
than I'd ever expected I would. She didn't
complain.

We came out into a fire lane — a broad
swathe that ran through the forest. It gave
a view down towards the trail again, and
as we cut across it I saw beyond the
forest, onto that bare valley beyond.

What I saw so startled me that I

gasped. Charmain's head came round at once and saw, too.

We didn't say anything, but hurried under cover again. For all across that valley we had seen men straggling towards the wooded area in small groups. It looked to me as if hundreds of Joanou supporters had been recruited and were now strung out in an effort to catch us.

It was chilling, that sight. There was something awfully relentless about the picture we'd both got. Like beaters flushing game for guns. There were so many, too, that we knew we didn't stand a chance.

We were being driven steadily towards the top of the mountain, and there comes a time on any mountain when you can't climb any higher. We climbed on, nevertheless. An instinct for self-preservation wouldn't let us give in, even though Charmain was back to exhaustion point again.

Again we had to cross a fire lane. We got across this safely without being seen, but we were just in time, for pursuers broke cover even as we re-entered the forest. It startled us to see the pursuit so near.

They had been so close that we had even seen the kind of dress they wore — young men with big thighs showing under small khaki drill shorts, the prevailing Cypriot fashion among the young. A few were without shirts. We even saw their faces, and there was laughter on one of them.

To the young men this was a game. Better than fox-hunting.

We turned, two fugitives striving unavailingly to escape from that relentless pursuit. In time we had to stop to get our breath. Anyway, Charmain had to stop.

She said, when she was recovering, wearily: 'Why don't you go on? You could keep ahead of them, Joe, because you look as strong as they are.'

I shook my head. I said: 'I don't go without you, honey. It's just not in the Heggy tradition to run out on a girl in distress I reckon.' I tried to make it flippant.

Her fingers gripped through my coat sleeve. She didn't say anything but I knew what she meant.

We went on climbing. We were going very slowly now. Behind us we heard heavy bodies blundering through occasional clumps of brushwood. We heard voices shouting. Each time that sound came to us I felt Charmain stiffen as if it came as a physical shock to her.

Then she began to cry. She was near the end of her tether now, I knew. It wasn't a nice way of crying, either. There were no tears. Just dry, rasping sobs. And I knew it was an expression of absolute physical terror.

I wiped away the sweat and asked: 'What are they shouting?'

She struggled on. Moaned: 'Joe, they can only kill you. But I'm a woman!'

I gripped her arm the tighter then. These Joanou supporters were young men. It was a game to them. But it was more than a game. When they got hold of Charmain they'd make sport with her. It was inevitable, with hot-blooded young men.

I was almost carrying her when the forest came to an end.

We walked right out of it. Suddenly we

were faced with an open expanse of at least a hundred yards — a stretch of rock and yellow soil burnt hard by the summer sun. There was no cover that I could see. Then I realised that the road came winding up from our right, almost level here and then went bearing right again up a hill that led to a second forest. We had to cross that roadway to get to the next patch of forest on this mountainside.

No one was in sight. We couldn't stay there, because we could hear that line of beaters advancing steadily up through the wood behind us. They couldn't have been more than a couple of hundred yards away, either, by the sound of their loud, confident young voices.

We started to run now. We just had to make that distant forest before we were seen. Once they saw us they'd be on to us in no time.

We were almost on to that road when a droning sound came to our ears from our right. Both of us knew at once what it was. A car was approaching.

I thought: Heck — Joanou!

And then frantically I looked for cover.

We were in a bad place. And then I saw a large drain let under the road at this point to take away flood water from the mountainside. I pushed Charmain into it and crouched by the entrance myself.

We listened, waiting. The noise grew louder, and then there was a crash of gears as the more level ground was reached. We felt the roadway vibrate and knew the car was passing overhead.

I lifted my eyes above the level of the roadway. Swirling dust fanned into them and I blinked. Then I saw that vehicle disappearing quickly up the road.

Charmain's head came round, and her eyes widened with wonder and shock. I was standing out there in the sunshine, exposed for all to see, and I was swearing as if I'd gone plain crazy.

She stumbled out and caught hold of my arm and dragged me across the road. She didn't understand. We ran into the wood and then I told her what I had seen.

We'd hidden from a police car!

'They were cops,' I groaned. 'Blast it, why didn't I think to check up before it passed us?'

We'd hidden away from safety. We could hear men's voices as they began to cross the trail preparatory to searching this next section of forest. All we could do was climb on and hope — though there was nothing we could hope for now.

Charmain gave in part way through that forest. I picked her up again, though I was dead beat myself. I felt as if I'd been half-carrying her all that morning.

I went along the face of the slope now, because I couldn't continue that climb with the girl in my arms. She lay with her head dropped back as if she hadn't any strength left at all.

I had to keep on carrying her, because I couldn't think of her in this condition being jumped on by that pack. They wouldn't bother about her exhaustion. She was a Cypriot girl and she had consorted with a foreigner.

So I stumbled on, within a few hundred yards of my own physical limits, too.

But within those few hundred yards the forest ended again. I came out of it and looked down and saw another surprising sight.

There was a shelf of rock protruding from the mountainside. It was too rocky for trees to grow upon. Everywhere on either side of that shelf was sheer drop to the valley far below.

And on that shelf I saw the outlines of a deserted army camp.

I went towards it, getting on to an old disused trail as I did so. I saw crumbling sandbags where machine gun posts had guarded the perimeter of the camp, and I saw tumbling buildings of stone with corrugated metal roofing now red with rust and dropping to pieces.

I walked into the camp. There were four rings of decaying sandbags where big ack-ack guns had been placed.

I looked around desperately for a place to hide, because now flight was over. Our only chance to escape was by hiding from our enemies.

I saw steps that led down into the rock and I guessed these would be underground ammunition dumps. But I couldn't go to earth like a rat. Down there I guessed there would be no alternative escape. Down there I would be trapped.

Voices rang out with sudden loudness. They were even closer than I'd imagined. I felt panicky. I stood there, holding the girl in my arms and I couldn't see a place where I could hide.

My mouth was so dry now that my tongue made rasping sounds as I tried to lick my lips. I wondered if there'd be water in this camp. I had a feeling that if only I could have a long, long drink I'd be able to face death without much worry. I was as bad as all that with thirst now.

Charmain didn't move. She was probably almost unconscious.

Then I saw a water tank built on top of a rocky promontory. That shattered my hopes of a water supply within this camp. I'd seen those things before.

This had been the water supply of the camp when it was in existence — only the water was brought from distant wells and pumped up into this rusting tank.

But it gave me an idea. Maybe because it was the most prominent feature in the camp it could be overlooked, just as I'd overlooked it at first. I began to use psychology in that desperate moment. I figured that it was instinct for fugitives to go underground, rather than perch themselves high up in the sky where they could be seen.

The psychology might have been faulty, but I saw no alternative and so I began to clamber up to where that tank was perched.

It was a grim climb, and I had to throw Charmain across my shoulder again to accomplish it. She revived in that position, at any rate sufficiently to groan and try to push her weight up off her stomach. I held on to her through her thin dress, and gasped for her to keep still.

All the time I climbed I was watching that tree line to my left. No one had appeared so far. But if I was seen before I got inside that tank . . . I reached the tank. Now I was screened if they did burst out into the open. The tank was higher than I'd expected, though I could look into it. But my strength had pretty well gone and I had to stand there and waste agonising minutes before I could heft Charmain over the edge and lower her into the rusty bottom. I expected her to go right through that sheet of rust, but it held.

I peered round the corner of the tank. Half a dozen young men, two with guns and the others with sticks, were streaming along the trail into the camp. They'd found us.

Even then I couldn't pull myself into the tank, not until I'd rested another minute and found the strength to drag myself over.

I flopped beside the girl — whacked. I just lay there and let the tiredness flow out of my muscles. I tried to quiet the labouring of my lungs, and in time I succeeded. Rust stuck to my face and to the hair on the back of my head where the sweat ran off in streams.

For just one minute that rusting iron tank was the most heavenly place I'd ever been in. Inside it I didn't need to push my flagging muscles any more.

And then all at once it ceased to be a refuge and became a torture chamber. The sun was over the rim and was beating down upon us, reflecting from the iron sides and adding to the heat within. We were cut off from any air currents, and within no time the place became intolerable. It was just an oven and two human beings were roasting within it.

Charmain was moaning, her eyes closed still. Her arms were flung wide from her body and her legs were apart so that no parts of herself were touching. In that heat when flesh touched flesh it was something that couldn't be borne.

I sat up wearily, and then I got on to my knees beside her and gently lifted her shoulders from the hot floor of the tank. I whispered hoarsely: 'You'll have to stand, baby. There's air above the level of this tank. Cooler air. It'll revive you.'

I mopped her streaming face with my handkerchief. It was a job I'd taken on quite a bit in the past hours, I realised. That face was dirty now, without any traces of make-up. It was beginning to look gaunt. And yet I liked that face then better than I'd ever liked it before.

Her distress brought out the compassion in me. I couldn't think of her as I'd once done. She was weaker than I and needed my strength, and right then I was going to give her every last ounce of it.

I pulled her upright. I figured that if we stood right at the back of the tank our heads would be above the level and yet not visible to the Cypriots down below.

I was right. We stood there in that blazing sunshine under that flawless blue sky and pine-scented air came and washed over our sweating heads. It was like nectar. If only we'd had a drink . . .

Charmain's eyes came open. She looked at me and then that smile came to her lips again. In adversity Charmain was finding courage. She could be gallant. My arm about her waist tightened. Only this time that tightening was comradely, affectionate.

I gave her a grin and said: 'We'll lick 'em yet.'

When she could stand I risked moving to the front of the tank and had a quick peep over.

When I turned away my eyes were closed for a second, as if to shut out the sight I had just seen. When I opened them Charmain was watching me.

She whispered: 'They're all there?'

231

I nodded. Men were streaming into that camp from all quarters. They had guessed we were hiding out there — probably they'd followed our trail over the last few yards. I hoped that trail didn't lead up this rocky slope to our hiding place.

I said, bluntly: 'There's dozens of them, honey, and they're taking this camp to pieces. They sure aim to get hold of us. That Joanou can call out a pretty mean mob when he likes.'

Charmain's eyes were too bright. She said, quickly:

'I don't want to fall into their hands, Joe. I know too much.'

Her hands gripped my arm. She was desperate.

'Joe, can't you end it all for me? Haven't you a knife or something?'

I slipped my arms round her then, trying to console her, trying to thrust back those fears that made her demand this horrifying thing. I told her: 'I don't carry weapons. I haven't got one. And I couldn't do it if I had.'

She spoke quickly, that note of hysteria

edging her voice. 'It'd be a kindness, Joe. You don't know our menfolk like I do. They'll think anything is justified. And they'll do it.' She moaned.

Her trembling hands took hold of my wrist. She put my hands round her throat. I looked into brown, terrified eyes. She whispered: 'Squeeze, Joe. End it all for me — now.'

I shook my head. I couldn't do anything like that. I'd have to hate someone a whole lot before I could kill them. I reckon I'd never hated anyone to that extent in my whole life.

She gave in then, and drooped, her head on my chest. Below our waistlines the airless heat inside that tank was appalling, but we had to stand it.

My eyes lifted hopelessly and looked up behind that camp. Trees grew there, too, those same pine trees that had hidden us for these past hours. I saw a scar a few hundred yards through them. For a time my eyes watched without seeing it. Then my head jerked erect and my eyes focused more closely.

I was beginning to recognise that scar.

Trees had been smashed aside, and I could see the gleaming whiteness where trunks had been ripped in half, Something gleamed within that patch.

I looked down onto the dark hair of Charmain and gently stroked it. I was feeling lower then than I've ever felt in my life.

We had gone through torments in the past fourteen or sixteen hours, blundering up hill and down dale and risking our necks in the darkness. And now, ironically, we were within a few hundred yards of where it had all started.

That gleaming thing amid those torn trees was the car that I had sent crashing off the roadway last night.

I thought of that crazy ex-editor Haverford. He'd probably gone under long ago. He was lucky. We still had to go through it, and it was going to be awfully painful for the pair of us.

The noise down below was intensified now. A new note was creeping into those excited tones. Now anger was replacing the eagerness that had been there before. I knew what that meant. The mob was feeling frustrated. The longer they were in finding us, the more cruel they would be.

Then I heard a car far below us, as it whined along a steep, rough track. I didn't dare look out to see whose car it was. It could be the police, searching the old road into the army camp.

But more likely it was the Joanou car, with Joanou himself inside. I figured that someone had got word to him that we had been cornered in the old army camp.

We stood there another half hour. By that time I reckon they'd taken the camp right apart three or four times. They hadn't found us, and yet they knew we were somewhere inside that camp. They must have known it because there was no escape beyond this rocky promontory — not a reasonable escape, with them so hard upon our heels as they had been.

It just didn't occur to them to look at the most prominent feature in the camp, this rusty old tank perched high up on a rocky cliff. My psychology had paid off . . . so far.

But it couldn't go on forever. In the end someone must have looked at that tank and thought: There's only one place left.

We heard feet scrabbling on the hillside below us. Charmain clung to me the closer in terror. We ducked into that airless heat of the old water tank.

There was a gasping sound as someone painfully clawed his way up to the edge of the water tank. Just one man.

I knelt against the side where the sounds came from. I was desperate.

I waited and then I saw a faded blue cloth, a headband like a turban. Then a head came into view. A thin brown face, unshaven, with brown eyes that looked in at first without any great hope of success and then with astonishment to find that a hunch had come off.

I gripped the peasant by the throat. I had to keep him quiet. My thumbs dug in. I didn't want to hurt him but . . . Charmain.

I think I could have done it, too. I think I could have kept him quiet and dragged him into that tank and so averted trouble.

Only, he must have been one of the men carrying guns. Maybe that was why he had had the courage to come up to that tank alone. Because he had a gun.

When I started to choke him unconscious, he let go of that gun, and I heard it clattering as it bounded down the rocky hillside.

It attracted attention. Someone looked. They saw their comrade with his head held over the edge of that old water tank, and the way he was fighting with his arms and kicking with his legs told a story. I heard a shout. And then a lot of shouting.

Then men were fighting to be first up that slope to get at that tank where the fugitives were hidden.

We'd lost the race. And we'd lost out in the end on our hiding place.

I let go of the Cypriot then. I didn't want to hurt him. I didn't want to hurt anybody, but I stood there and I was determined that any man who tried to get in at us would stop my fists.

All at once men were looking over the edge of that tank, so that we were ringed round by excited faces.

I had an impression of young faces, eager-eyed, excited and triumphant. And there were dozens of them around that tank. There wasn't a chance for us.

Charmain stood up by my side then. She was no less terrified, I could see, but with her last strength she summoned up her pride and stood by me with dignity. I saw it, and even then I had time to approve and to say to her: 'Charmain, you're a honey. That's the way to face 'em!'

The shouting rose to a crescendo, as everyone told everyone else to get into the tank and pull us out. All at once a flood of men came over. I pushed Charmain back against a wall and I went crazy, lashing out with my fists, trying to hurt but above all trying to keep them away from the girl.

It was awful, fighting inside that tank. There was red iron dust kicked up and floating over us and it got up my nose and in my mouth, and they were too dry already to take kindly to that powder. The sun's heat was terrific, especially with all those hot bodies crowding upon us.

They were hitting out at me with their sticks and gun butts. And they weren't missing.

I was hitting some of them — hurting, too, I knew but I couldn't hold out against all their numbers. I couldn't stand up against that savage fury of blows that assailed me, that stunned me, that blinded me and sent me down to the floor of that tank.

Even then the sadism was not restrained. I couldn't see, my eyes puffed up from the many blows they'd taken. Blood ran from my nose and I tasted it in my gasping mouth. They struck at me, shouting, because you have to work up an anger when you are being cruel to a helpless victim. Their heavy boots kicked into me.

And then there was a reprieve. Charmain saved me from further punishment.

I got one eye partly open then, lying on that drumming steel floor. I saw them grab Charmain from behind me. She was lifted like a shuttlecock.

She screamed, and at that there was a quick, whipping roar of laughter. I knew what that laugh meant.

I knew what was in their minds. And I could only lie and watch because I'd taken too much punishment in that last couple of minutes. Then I began to swing a rifle and I don't know where the strength came from.

When I'd finished I started to crawl out of the tank. None of them tried to stop me. They were down in a corner, stunned and bleeding.

But I couldn't have saved Charmain.

Then I saw Joanou, running up. I don't know what he was intending. Maybe to have his share of the fun. Maybe to establish some sort of order.

I don't know.

All I knew was that I wanted to kill him then. He, that cowardly man, had been the cause of too much violence, of too many deaths.

But I couldn't get to him, either.

Then there was a scream from the road-way below us, just as I saw a movement from the brushwood that hedged the camp.

My eyes swung involuntarily. A man — a Cypriot — was signalling down on the roadway. I guessed what that signal meant. Danger. It must have been that police car again.

Joanou was shouting orders. I knew what they'd be, too. Keep quiet everyone. Get under cover. We'll start all over again when the cops turn round and go back. But don't let them see you.

They were going to see *me*!

And then I saw that I wasn't needed . . . yet. I saw that movement again. Someone had come down through those trees and was now staggering into the camp. An awful sight. A bloody wreck of a man.

Peter John Haverford.

He was right there among those men, and he was past the crazy line now. He was a complete nut and you could see it in those wild, staring eyes.

He had seen Charmain in the grip of these men, and she was lifted out of the tank, incapable of resistance. Greedy hands clutched her body and gripped into her limbs.

She went out feet first, her hair, long and black, trailing over the side.

She couldn't struggle against all those many hands. That must have been the horrifying part about it.

Someone shouted an order. The last

two eager young men to climb out of the tank were halted on the edge. They sat back and looked at me with anger in their eyes.

I got it. They'd been told to watch me, and they didn't want to. They wanted to go down and share that sport with their inflamed, eager comrades.

One had a gun — an old sporting gun but lethal at close quarters. The other had a long forked stick.

They were both watching over the edge of the tank, their eyes drinking in that scene, never missing a detail . . . satisfying themselves vicariously. I rolled and came on to my knees and it took a lifetime to do it and it seemed as if it drained away every last bit of strength.

But then strength came back with anger, and I swayed to my feet.

The stubble-faced young Cypriot with the gun turned his shiny brown face and shouted something at me. His gun muzzle menaced me. I took no notice of it.

I pushed my way to the edge of that tank. Below a flood of men surged around the door of a falling army building.

I heard Charmain begin to scream again.

That scream brought the Cypriot's head round, the one with the gun. The other fellow was already looking, his hands gripping the edge of the tank.

I just took that gun from him by the barrel. It blew off and tore away my sleeve, but it didn't hurt me, he couldn't stand that, either. He came towards them, and his revolver was shooting. Shooting slowly. Not in a hurry to get it over.

I thought maybe he was counting. Maybe he was trying to save the last two bullets. One for Charmain. One for himself.

I saw those Cypriots fall back and begin to dash away. They had guns but they weren't gunmen and hadn't the instinct to use them right then. Anyway, somehow a revolver is a more frightening weapon than a shotgun. A revolver isn't any use for anything except killing men.

Haverford was trying to kill them then. He wasn't hitting all the time, but some of his bullets couldn't miss. Joanou stopped one between the eyes. Men were screaming in pain and panic and that added to the confusion. There was dust everywhere as their scurrying feet sent it up in clouds. They were shouting hoarsely, and then sheer panic set in. That must have been when the police came falling out of their car. Just a few cops. Maybe three or four. But those uniforms were enough to start a rout.

I'd fallen out of the tank now. I'd fallen down that hillside, too. Because I knew what I had to do.

They'd left Charmain. I could see her inside the open doorway of that old hut, turning her head slowly, despairingly, to look out towards us.

She saw that shambling wreck of a man, a man who had somehow survived an appalling car crash. Who had lived when by rights he ought to have died, but who hadn't long on earth even at that.

He was reeling towards the door. He gripped it. Then he stood there, sagging.

I got to my feet and staggered towards them. I couldn't see clearly for the sweat and blood in my puffed-up eyes. I wasn't much better than Haverford right then.

Everyone seemed to be running away from us. All except a cop. But he was too far away. And there was a fat little man with him.

I just saw that. And then I saw Haverford's hand lift that gun and point it at her.

At Charmain.

At a girl who deserved a lot.

But I couldn't let her go out this way. We had suffered together. We'd been comrades for too long.

Or maybe I just felt protective.

I fell and my hand gripped that wrist and my weight pulled him toppling over. We lay there, panting and glaring at each other, and I still held his wrist with that gun clasped in his long fingers.

He started to bring the muzzle round. He wanted to kill me, because he guessed that I'd had more than he had. That I'd won Charmain's favours. That she liked me and had no time for him.

I thought I hadn't the strength, but when the blue eye of death was coming round to look me between the eyes, I found all the strength I needed. I swung over and my balled fist hit him in the stomach. He passed out. The gun fell from his hand and he wasn't to be feared any more.

I went crawling in to Charmain, leaving Peter John Haverford, killer of Christopholou and that poor bus driver, to be picked up by those cops. Just now I wanted to go in and tell Charmain not to worry.

'Everything's all right, honey,' I croaked, kneeling beside her. 'It's all over now. They're just being rounded up.'

She didn't seem to understand, but then her hand took mine and held it. A shadow blocked the daylight and with a curious sense of fitness I pulled the tattered remnants of her dress around her.

A little apple of a man was trying to help me to my feet. He was saying: 'You've been having quite a time, Mr. Heggy.'

It made me grin. That was a superb understatement. Then I looked at the Armenian dick and I thought I had never seen a more welcome face. It was red and beamed with friendliness.

He was saying: 'I didn't want you to think I was a heel, Mr. Heggy. Honest, I had lost my money. But I found it. I want to pay you back.'

They were helping Charmain up. She wouldn't let them take her away from me. We were both being supported out and down to the car. Cypriot police were there, helpful and kindly.

Keremetlian was exhilarated. 'I saw you go off from the hotel with that man with glasses. Some time later the police started to ask us if we'd seen that man with glasses, who'd been on the bus. I knew then you'd been forced to go away. So we started searching the hills because I had seen you head that way.'

I said: 'Girais, you're a pal. I don't know what I'd have done if you hadn't started this search.'

But I knew.

★ ★ ★

Lavinia was giving B.G. hell. I never saw such a change in a woman. B.G. got me in a corner and said, haggardly: 'She's jealous. She says I make eyes at all the women. It's . . . hell, Joe.'

He mopped his streaming face. His eyes behind his tycoon's glasses were desperate.

I'd seen a ring on Lavinia's maidenly finger. I held out my hand. 'What can I do? You go and stick your neck in a noose. Why ask me to get it out for you?'

'I must have been mad.' B.G. rocked in agony. 'She was so nice, and before I knew what I was doing I was trying to make amends for — for — '

'You don't need to tell me.' I flipped a bandaged paw. It reminded me that I was a mass of aches in every part of my body. 'You thought you'd treated her wrongly back in Istanbul and you thought a ring would make it right for you.'

I started to go towards the stairs. I told him he was a sap. Love 'em and leave 'em, I was telling him. That's all Lavinia wanted, anyway.

It took me a long time to get up those stairs. Try climbing stairs when your legs won't bend at the knees. Mine wouldn't.

They'd got too many bandages on. The entire hotel watched me stagger up like a gouty man, I was sure.

At the head of the stairs I met Miss Paterson and her good companion, Miss George. It was the first time they'd seen me since the hospital stopped putting medicated tape on me. They were concerned.

I said: 'Sorry I can't stop, ladies. I've got someone to see.'

I couldn't keep away from Charmain. We had suffered too much together. I went in to her. She was lying on top of her bed for coolness. They'd stuck her in an unbecoming hospital gown, maybe because her own pyjamas wouldn't fit over the bandages.

Her hands were taped with pink medicated plaster, and her feet were big bundles of white bandage. I reckoned there were odd yards of plaster underneath that nightie, too, but it was a chaste affair and didn't show anything.

I didn't look, anyway. I was looking at Charmain's face. She was propped up against snowy white pillows that showed the luxuriant abundance of that glossy black hair of hers. The colour had come back to her face. Lipstick and carmine, I mean.

But she looked good. Suddenly healthy again, and as full of life and vitality as ever she'd been. Attractive in the way that few women are attractive to me.

And yet she wasn't trying to attract me.

I sat on the edge of her bed and looked out over the balcony at the glorious blue Mediterranean and the distant mountains of Anatolia. I saw her smile out of the corner of my eyes. She was looking at me whimsically.

'Trying to think of something bright to say, Joe?'

I turned to her and shrugged. Then I put my hand on her bandaged one. 'All I can say surprisingly, Charmain, is — it's been nice knowing you.'

Colour pulsed into her cheeks at that. Her big brown eyes looked brighter. 'You really mean that?'

'Honey, I do.' I was genuine about it, too.

Her bandaged fingers clutched my

hand. Her eyes closed quickly as if against a wave of pain.

I said: 'You still want to go to America, baby?'

She looked out of the window. Said: 'Cyprus is no place for me any more, Joe. It's such a little place. I can't live down what's happened. I don't want to, knowing my responsibility for things.'

I said: 'Okay, I'll fix for you to go to Detroit. My firm will guarantee you a job and then you'll be all right. You won't need to worry. You'll get by in America. Maybe meet a nice guy and settle down.'

There were tears through those nearly closed eyelids.

She whispered: 'There's only one nice guy I want.'

And, with a laugh that broke a little: 'You're as bad as your boss. Saving himself up for when the right woman comes along.'

I hadn't thought of it that way before.

I stood up. I just felt I had to go down and have a drink, because I didn't like to stand up a girl and remain in her company for long. At the door I paused. I felt really friendly towards her, though I knew Miss George, at any rate, would say she didn't deserve it.

Charmain's voice came after me. 'Joe.'

I turned. She was smiling gallantly. This was one time in her life that she hadn't got what she wanted, and yet she didn't mind . . . much,

I said: 'Yeah?'

'I'm going to have a lifetime of regrets now, Joe.'

'Such as?'

'I'm going to wish I'd always been a good girl and then I might have made you.'

I had to make a wisecrack as I went out, though I felt like a louse. But I didn't dare let the atmosphere get any more sentimental.

I said: 'The hell, baby. You've got it wrong. If you'd been a good girl Joe P. Heggy wouldn't even have looked at you.'

We do hope that you have enjoyed reading this large print book.

Did you know that all of our titles are available for purchase?

We publish a wide range of high quality large print books including:
Romances, Mysteries, Classics
General Fiction
Non Fiction and Westerns

Special interest titles available in large print are:
The Little Oxford Dictionary
Music Book, Song Book
Hymn Book, Service Book

Also available from us courtesy of Oxford University Press:
Young Readers' Dictionary
(large print edition)
Young Readers' Thesaurus
(large print edition)

For further information or a free brochure, please contact us at:
Ulverscroft Large Print Books Ltd.,
The Green, Bradgate Road, Anstey,
Leicester, LE7 7FU, England.
Tel: (00 44) **0116 236 4325**
Fax: (00 44) **0116 234 0205**

MAN OF TWO WORLDS

John Russell Fearn

Walter Cardish was a very ordinary, somewhat downtrodden individual. But, following an incredible accident, he recovers in hospital and finds that he has been granted the power of seeing into the future. Assuming the identity of 'The Great Volta: Prognosticator' he amasses a fortune, and a reputation as a seer. But his activities also create enemies, and soon one of them tries to kill him, and the implacable workings of his strange destiny close in upon him inexorably . . .

SHERLOCK HOLMES AND THE CROSBY MURDERS

Gary Lovisi

The glamorous actress Susan Copely is being persecuted — and the reason lies in the events surrounding the wreck of the *Sophy Anderson* two decades before . . . A well-regarded business-man appears to have brutally stabbed his wife to death, and then suffocated their two small children before fleeing their home. But Holmes, deploying his unique investigative methods, is set upon proving otherwise . . . Finally, a most singular narrative from Mycroft Holmes at last sheds light upon what truly happened at the Reichenbach Falls that fateful day in 1891 . . .

THE CHRONICLES OF SHERLOCK HOLMES

Paul D. Gilbert

Dr John Watson reveals unchronicled cases only previously alluded to: The Baron Maupertuis, The Remarkable Disappearance of James Phillimore, The Aluminium Crutch, The Abominable Wife, The Cutter *Alicia*, The Red Leech and The Mumbling Duellist . . . What is the connection between an impoverished dowager, an attempt on Mycroft's life and Holmes's deadliest adversary? Can Holmes discover if a ship really disappeared in a patch of mist or is his client's father insane? And who or what is the red leech?

NAPLES, OR DIE!

David Bingley

1943. The British 8th Army had crossed over from Messina to Reggio and 'Scoop' Britwell, a fighting war correspondent, suffered from battle fatigue. Always on the lookout for his brother, Captain 'Tufty' Britwell of the Home Counties Commandos, he's captured by the Germans where he befriends Lieutenant Rawson, an L.C.T. skipper, and Dusty Lewis, a Pioneer. When he is released by British troops, 'Scoop' finally catches up with 'Tufty' and together they face the fighting in Naples . . .

THE ATLANTIC TUNNEL

John Russell Fearn

Deep beneath the floor of the Atlantic Ocean, scientists and engineers attempt the most daring and audacious scientific project of all time: the construction of an undersea tunnel between Great Britain and Canada; linking Land's End with Labrador. Canadian and British teams work simultaneously at either end, to converge in the middle. Using scientific methods to fight the crushing pressure and geological and marine perils involved, the brave workers face a far greater hazard — the danger within — from saboteurs!